The BRIDE of AMBROSE
and Other Stories

The BRIDE of AMBROSE and Other Stories

Castle Freeman

The following stories have been previously published, in slightly different form: "Seven Prophecies of Egypt" in *fiction international,* "That Is No Country For Old Men" in *New England Review and Breadloaf Quarterly,* "My Life On The Snowplow" and "Before He Went Out West" in *The Massachusetts Review,* and "Dreaming of Africa" in *The Iowa Review.*

Library of Congress Cataloging-in-Publication Data

Freeman, Castle, 1944–
 The bride of Ambrose and other stories.

 I. Title.
PS3556.R3838B7 1987   813'.54   86–31522
ISBN 0–939149–01–X

Manufactured in the United States of America
FIRST EDITION

For
A.C.F.

Contents

1

Seven PROPHECIES of EGYPT

The last oxen in the Town of Ambrose, Vermont, came at the town's hire in the summer of 1940 to haul Nelson Pettibone's forfeited cabins from Ambrose village to wherever any of their new owners wanted them to sit. They were Murray's team. When Murray brought them to Ambrose, he didn't go by the highway. He drove his team through the woods over Old Egypt.

Old Egypt was the name of a road. It had been out of use for a hundred years at the time, and the woods had taken it over almost completely. Murray's beasts came slowly over that useless track, their heads down, though they were pulling light, their forequarters swinging easily from side to side; Murray walking on their right, holding a branch which he rested on the near ox's hump.

Old Egypt was hard to find. People who didn't live near it no longer knew there was a road up there. Murray's drive may have been the last time Old Egypt was put to any good use. I use it, but not for anything that needs doing, and hunters use it. But it is thirty-five years since Old Egypt has known the weight and pull of a real job of work: when Murray and his oxen hauled Nelson's little cabins out of Ambrose Center, for ten cents on the tax dollar.

★ ★ ★

The cabins came from a tourist camp Nelson started outside the village. He might have made a success of the place, but the selectmen threatened to close him down because he wasn't insured. Nelson went before the selectmen and stripped them up one side and down the other, but, in the event, he capitulated. He never got the insurance the selectmen required, he never tried to run his place in defiance of the selectmen. He chucked the whole operation, and the selectmen sold off the cabins for unpaid taxes. That was in 1938, '39, and '40.

"Selectmen in these little towns," Nelson would say, "take an oath of office to be against anything that's better than what they have always been used to. They just cannot stand for anyone to do anything in their town except leave, or milk cows all his life, or kill himself working in the woods, like them and everyone else they know. Let anybody try something a little new, that those fellows don't know everything about, and, unless he goes broke pretty quickly, they begin to worry. What's more, if he not only doesn't go broke but looks like he might be getting by, they fall all over themselves to find a way to bring him down so they can plow under whatever he started to do and plant grass on it, and start forgetting it ever happened."

The board of selectmen believed Nelson Pettibone was someone who thought the law didn't mean
him, who thought his hopes and plans were special,
were so much more original than the hopes and plans of
others that they had to be exempt from the limits which
others' hopes and plans must observe. Ed MacBean said,
"We knew we weren't going to get anywhere with Nelson. All he could think of was how smart he was to get
people to pay cash to stay on property that, as long as
Nelson or anyone else could remember, wasn't of any
use except to grow poor hay. He had them paying him
money to stay there. It wasn't much money, but it was
easy money. Nelson couldn't see past how easy it was.
And that is why we knew we would never get anywhere
with him. He didn't want to make money, or get rich, or
chisel the tourists. If he had, he would have straightened
out. But all he wanted was a lazy, easy time, and so,
when we read the ordinance to him, he just went away.
When fellows like Nelson finally figure out that some
people don't work as hard as others for their living, they
get excited; but when they realize later that, still, almost
everybody has to do a few things he doesn't like, they
get mad. They feel they have been cheated."

Nelson wanted a better life, only not too much
better; a different life, anyway, but not too different. He
wanted to be a proprietor, a taker-in of money, like a
merchant. He was one of those country men—children
of small farmers, country artisans, and woodsmen—
whose adult ambition it was to spend their lives tending
store. There are not so many with that ambition any
more, but there used to be thousands whose experience
of the farm or the shop around which they grew up was
such that, grown, they wanted nothing better than to

move down into a little town and get their living sitting behind a counter. To Nelson it seemed that the tourist trade, in 1938 undreamed of by all but him, would give an easy way into that life. For him, no premises to keep up, no inventory to keep track of. His stock in trade would be a few cheap acres beside the highway and his customers tired motorists who, at that time, had no place within thirty miles to stop at except his.

His first spring, Nelson bought five acres on the main road at the end of the village. It had been a hayfield, but Nelson ran a drive from the road up the center of the five acres, and then set up sawhorses, boards, old railroad ties, 55-gallon drums, and other junk about the land to mark off ten plots. On each plot he put a circle of fieldstones for a fireplace. Then he put up a signboard down on the road.

PETTIBONE'S

WAYSIDE CAMPGROUND

Nightly & Weekly Rates

Cooking Facilities

He charged fifty cents a night and three dollars for a week.

Was Nelson a prophet of Ambrose's destiny, of the whole state's destiny? Did he, even before Ambrose had come out of its hundred years' agrarian enchantment, envision a time when sixty-five cents of every dollar taken in in these parts would come from those very tourists whose fathers he had tried to lure? In however botched and futile a way, was Nelson Ambrose's first modern man? I don't think so. If Nelson had a picture of the future, it was of him sitting on a camp stool in front of his tent, passing the time of day with his tourists and laughing up his sleeve at his friends and neighbors who still pulled in the old traces with nothing changed from year to year but the date.

At the end of his first summer on the campground he closed up and took down his sign. For the season, he said, though he admitted he hadn't made any money. In fact, he was behind. Not so many motorists had stopped. And then, not all of the ones who did stop paid up on leaving, so Nelson had begun collecting rent in advance, which cost him some business. The work and expenses involved in running the place, which Nelson had figured for nil, turned out to be not large, but not nil either. He found he had to supply firewood, for one thing, and water; otherwise campers would wander into the woods around Nelson's five acres, cutting the smaller trees and filling their kettles at the brooks. Those woods weren't part of the property, and Nelson's neighbors complained right off.

Nelson couldn't understand the complaints at first, but then, he said, he began to see the handwriting on the wall.

"You ask yourself a minute," he said. "You ask yourself a minute who these people are that, the first time one of my campers' kids puts his foot on their land, start to bawl and raise hell. Well, one of them is Mrs. Hunter. She doesn't like all those people—get that: 'All those people?'—who are taking water out of her brook. Hell, she's eighty-five. She had probably forgotten there was a brook in there until somebody reminded her. The other one is Paul Roberts. He doesn't like them in the brook, and he doesn't like them cutting firewood in his woods. He says the noise bothers him: dogs barking, and the rest. Yet he is half a mile away, and he's got four or five dogs of his own that the whole town can hear any time somebody walks in the road past his house. But let somebody from my camp go in there and pick up a dead branch, or laugh out loud, and: 'Oh, God. Oh, Lord, my firewood, my ears. Oh, God!'

"You ask yourself, and you see, it isn't the brook and the wood and the noise that they don't like or that is bothering them. It's the idea that somebody is trying something new and bringing in outsiders. Some of them might decide they like it here. They might decide to stay. They might even spend some money. Wouldn't that be awful? I don't wonder at Old Lady Hunter, but I thought Roberts had more on the ball."

It looked like Nelson was going to have to get in his own water and wood for the campground. When he did, though, and then tried to charge a little money for water and wood, he found some of his campers would pick up and leave. He had supposed anyone who could afford a car, and the time to pack his wife and kids all over the countryside, would open up easily for anything he really needed. He found he was wrong.

The campground was a dead letter, but Nelson had the enterprise to get in a little deeper. The second spring, as soon as the snow was out of Nelson's five acres, he was out there with a helper and a stack of lumber. By May he had put up ten cabins, one in each of his old campsites. The cabins were dark, damp, and small—ten by twelve with one window—and they were made up of rough two-by-fours with clapboards tacked over them outside, and, inside, walls of some kind of cheap composition sheet. Stiff tents, is what Nelson's cabins were.

Each cabin sat on four little piles of bricks at the corners. Since the biggest piece in any of them was a two-by-four, they were all more or less rickety: you could take hold of a corner of any of them and move the whole structure. Each cabin had a small oil heater, two cots, a table, a chair, a washstand, a pot. Sanitary arrangements were five or six little shacks backed into the trees on the edge of the property. They called Nelson's place 'Piss-in-the-Woods Cabins.'

Nelson painted the ten cabins green. He hung up a new sign on the road.

PETTIBONE'S

GREEN MOUNTAIN CABINS

Double Accommodations Available

Furnished

Cooking Facilities

Nightly & Weekly Rates

He quadrupled his prices and waited for trade.

It was soon clear Nelson had a better thing in the cabins than he had ever had in the campground. For a few days around the Fourth of July all ten cabins were occupied (the campground had never filled up), and Nelson had to make a *No Vacancy* sign to hang under his main sign. He himself set up a big army tent in a corner of the property.

Nelson walked about among the cabins, saw that everything was all right, dropped a load of wood, told his guests where they might see a deer, broke up dog fights, accepted a bottle of beer, took in his money.

The tourists who stopped at Nelson's: hot, sweaty, crabby families from Fall River and Bridgeport, from New York and New Jersey. They rolled into Nelson's old hayfield at the end of a ten- or twelve-hour drive: bored kids, tired wives, sticky seats—the pioneers of the Manifest Destiny of American Leisure. And Nelson was there waiting for them.

"Drive it right over there to Number Four. In the corner."

Bumping over the meadow. Engine off. The kids are out, they run into Number Four. Nelson walks up as they unload. Something runs out from under the cabin. "Looks like a kitty cat," Nelson says. (Skunk, it was.)

"Sure, we see deer up here all the time. They come out right behind your cabin. At dusk. You'll see them if you're quiet. Saw a good buck right here last deer season, didn't have my gun, though."

★ ★ ★

Ed MacBean was one of the Ambrose selectmen. He looked Nelson up one day. "What exactly are you up to there, Nelson?" MacBean said.

"Up where?"

"Those cabins. What are you doing up there?"

"Doing business, Ed," Nelson said. "Doing pretty well."

"Well, all right," MacBean said, "but is that just a temporary thing up there, or do you intend to set up permanently? Because if it's permanent—well, even if it isn't—there are some things we need to get straightened out. We're a little worried. For instance, what have you got for insurance up there? What if you had a fire?"

"I don't worry about it," Nelson said. "I don't need insurance."

"You do," MacBean said. "You haven't thought it out. All you can think of is how smart you were to throw up those piddling little shacks for next to nothing and call them tourist cabins. If one of them burned down, you say, why, it won't cost you but about five dollars to build another. But what if one of them burned down with someone inside it, for instance? One of your guests? They could sue you, any of them that were left. And if you couldn't compensate, and if they had a good lawyer, they possibly could sue the town. It's happened other places, Nelson. You need liability insurance. I think you'd better look into it."

"What if I decide I don't need liability," Nelson asked.

"We might have to close you down. We don't want to do that. But if this business you have got up there is a business just like any other business in town, then it has got to act like a business just like any other business in town, and you have to get some things straightened out, including your liability arrangements."

"How could you close me down?" Nelson asked.

"We think we can close you just for not having the liability insurance," MacBean said. "But anyway, we can close you for being a hazard to public health."

"Oh, hell," Nelson said.

"Well, Nelson, Roberts says the brook up there is running a little rank." MacBean rubbed his chin. "Down to Roberts's it's got a head on it like a glass of warm beer, he says."

"Oh, hell, Ed," Nelson said.

"Look into that liability," MacBean said.

Nelson called on an insurance company. He described his property, his business, his needs. The agent quoted Nelson a certain figure. At the next meeting of the board of selectmen Nelson stood up.

"Now you can sit here and talk about your duty to the taxpayers and what might happen if something else happened if some other thing happened. But there isn't any place where it says the town has a responsibility to taxpayers to make it impossible to conduct an honest business in the town. There isn't any such responsibility. And all I've got to say is, if the selectmen or anybody else can say somebody can't conduct an honest business, then that's a goddamned hell of a situation. And that's all we have got here. And that's all I have got to say. You have to decide whether you want to force me out of my own business for some insurance you know I don't need, but I don't have to wait on you."

Nelson missed his taxes on the cabin property that summer. MacBean and the selectmen waited. At the time a good quarter of the tax accounts in Ambrose were delinquent. The third spring, Nelson never opened up the cabins. He had a night watchman job in Brattleboro. He lived in a rooming house there. MacBean looked him up again. How would it be if the town took on the property, sold off whatever it could, and cancelled Nelson's taxes?

"Take it away, Ed," Nelson said.

MacBean went to see Murray, the teamster.

"What will you take to bring your team over sometime next month and haul those little cabins?" he asked Murray.

"Haul them where?"

"To wherever anyone who bought one wanted you to," MacBean said.

"I could be hauling them until winter that way," Murray said. "I can work two days for you."

"You will be done in two days."

"Fifteen dollars," Murray said.

★ ★ ★

One of Nelson Pettibone's old Piss-in-the-Woods Cabins is my toolshed. Of the ten cabins that Nelson put up in 1939 at least half a dozen are still around the village, including mine and a cabin which Murray and his animals dragged up here over Old Egypt and in which Mariani, my neighbor, now keeps chickens. For cheap and hasty construction, Nelson's work has held up pretty well. It would make a piece of archaeology to trace—in today's sheds, camps, coops, privies, and shacks—components originating in Nelson's premature attempt to cash in on the tourist trade. You would have to do some looking around to find them all.

My house stands beside Old Egypt, halfway between Ambrose village and the top of the hill. The house is mostly sound, though the sills on the north side need attention; from beneath the bottom trim outside you can scoop handfuls of rotten wood. The sills have been rotting away for a hundred and seventy-five years, so they can rot on for another year or two until I can afford to have them replaced. There is that kind of fool's comfort in a very old house.

Old Egypt passes my dooryard and goes on up the hill into the woods. That road is one of my interests. It is older than the oldest house in the town, having been cleared out at the time of the first settlements. It went from Ambrose village up the side and around the top of a minor elevation called Burnt Hill and down the other side to Egypt, a smaller settlement now long since vanished. When Old Egypt was built there was another road to Egypt village which took a longer course through bottomlands around the base of the hill. Originally, Old Egypt was the main road, and the road that went below the hill was little used; but it happened that the lower road became a considerable highway, while Old Egypt was given up to brush.

For a century Old Egypt had been an important thoroughfare: it was on the Brattleboro Stage, and a historical account of the town mentions goods and ordnance moving over it bound for Lake Champlain in the War of 1812. But better roads were built, going to better places. At the time of the Civil War Old Egypt was just a farmers' road, and when the farmers packed up, it began to settle back into the forest from which their great-grandfathers had brought it forth.

By the turn of the century the farms outlying Ambrose village had mostly been abandoned. The village had pulled in upon itself, and the roads leading out, including Old Egypt, were nothing more than vague ways through the woods where nobody went. It was almost as though people were afraid of the woods that closed Old Egypt in. A crazy woman who stole children was supposed to live up Burnt Hill, and in the June 16, 1904 edition of the *Vermont Phoenix,* published in Brattleboro, there is a curious account of an Ambrose man who, coming over Old Egypt, met with a talking bear.

The *Phoenix* correspondent plays the story for laughs, rather heavily, identifying the townsman as "a laborer named O'Toole" and implying that he was drunk when he spoke with the bear in the woods above Ambrose. That was inevitable: no New England journalist at the time could resist the Alcoholic Irishman. What does the story really tell?

O'Toole was a sawyer. That June of 1904 he worked not in Ambrose, but in Egypt village, and he walked through the woods three miles each way to and from the sawmill along Old Egypt. From the outlying houses of Egypt village three miles over the hill to O'Toole's there was no house, and no opening in the woods.

The bear was to one side of the old roadway, and in the early-summer dusk, O'Toole thought it was a calf until it came into the path. "Better days are coming," the bear said.

O'Toole didn't say anything. The bear kept at a distance of a few yards from him and occupied itself in searching about near the ground, peering and poking among the low cover. But all the time it was undoubtedly speaking. It spoke, in a low clear voice, of the period a hundred years before, when the hill they stood on was an open pasture; although the bear could hardly have been around in those days. Certainly, no bear that did not have the power of speech has ever lived so long.

"Sheep," the bear was saying. "They used to run sheep all over that hill. It was all pasture. There wasn't a tree or a weed higher than a sheep could crop it. There was a woodlot at the top, but the rest was open down to the bottom except for haymows and fields below. Look at it now. No sunlight can get in there—you can't see twenty feet into the woods. It was as clear as a fairground," the bear said. "They have let it go."

"What are you?" O'Toole asked the bear.

"They've let it go," the bear went on, "and they wonder why everybody is working for somebody else and nobody has anything of his own or any pride. Everybody has a boss, and nobody is free, and they don't have anything, even so. They stopped selling their rightful products and sold their own lives instead, and their health and precious time."

"What do you want?" O'Toole asked.

"But it's going to turn around. They will open up the woods again, they will clear them right out. You will be able to see around the country from up here again. There will be houses all over this hillside. No sheep, but gardens, orchards, grass, and pasture. Everybody will have his own place and live as equals in the open, and not go sneaking in and out of mills and factories in the dark."

That is all that is supposed to have passed between the bear and O'Toole. Nobody in Ambrose today has any recollection of either of them. O'Toole may have been drunk, as the newspaper story of his adventure suggests; he may have been lying. O'Toole may not have existed at all: the *Phoenix*'s editor had a paper to get out, and in those days reporters weren't shy about inventing, out of thin air, stories they knew no one would ever believe in the first place or ever disprove.

And, indeed, even supposing the meeting of
O'Toole and the bear to have been as reported, the bear
doesn't show as much of a prophet. Burnt Hill is as
wooded and worthless today as it was in O'Toole's
time—more so, for Egypt village, at its foot, is now part
of the same abandonment the bear deplored. They have
let it go, too. In 1940, when Murray drove his oxen
through the woods to Ambrose to haul Nelson Pettibone's cabins, the going was hard even for animals.
Murray had to cut a couple of good-sized trees and chop
a lot of brush to make his way.

★ ★ ★

Murray brought his team over one day in August. He
could, he said, take just that day and the next on Nelson's cabins, for he had another job after that near his
own place. Murray worked on jobs that tractors couldn't
do, or he worked for people who didn't want tractors.
He was glad to have work in the summer, as his team
was hired mostly during the winter for woods work in
snow.

He got three boys to help him. They jacked one
of Nelson's cabins up off its foundations, cleared the
foundations out, and rolled a flatbed underneath. Then
they lowered the cabin onto the bed and guyed it down
with ropes. They hitched up the team and started. The
oxen pulled up, and the whole arrangement bumped off
on its way, the cabin lurching from side to side, Murray
up front beside the animals, and the boys hanging onto
the ropes and the cabin itself, trying to keep it aboard
and trying to keep it from falling apart.

They hauled several cabins to places around the
village, and then on the second afternoon they loaded

the last two on at once and rolled back up Old Egypt, which was Murray's way home. When Murray spoke to his team he said, "All right, Smart." Smart was one of the oxen's names, evidently. The other one didn't seem to have a name.

Murray unloaded one cabin at Mariani's, down the hill, and the last one at what has become my house. Then his three helpers walked back down to the village, Murray took his animals back over the hill. His oxen had left Ambrose village for the last time.

2

The RIDE

The helper, Toby, was getting done putting gas in Mr. Oates's truck when a silver Porsche came up top the hill by Raymond's, shifted, and blew it off up the road and out of sight.

All *right,* Toby thought.

"Sewing machine," Oates said. He had been watching Toby fill his gas. "Little sewing machine, there," he said in the noise of the Porsche going away up the road. "Take your toys someplace else, why don't you?"

That's no toy, Toby thought. "Ten fifty," he told Oates.

"Write it up for me," Oates said. He climbed back into his truck and took it like a bucket of water out into the road and away from the station.

Toby was by himself at Raymond's until ten. He went back inside the station and got out the accounts to write Oates up. What toy? he thought.

Toby liked the Porsche. He liked the BMW, the Alfa. He did not like the Trans Am or the Camaro. He did not like any of the Japs. In short, he wasn't attracted to those automobiles that he—with luck he knew he wouldn't have—might someday expect to own. In short, he admired a machine that looked like income as well as rpms.

Bland was meant to be the night man with Toby, but sometimes he only came in to close up. Tonight Bland came at ten. He had a sandwich in a paper bag for Toby. Toby paid Bland for the sandwich. He ate it with a drink out of their machine. Bland sat at the desk in the station tapping on the edge of the desk top with his fingers, bobbing his head, and going *boo-boo-boo* silently with his lips.

Toby got his coat. "Where are you going, Rowena's?" Bland asked him.

"Yes," Toby said.

"Rowena's, huh?" Bland said. He thumped the desk top faster. "Well, you look out, boy. You watch yourself."

"Oh, yes," Toby said.

"How are you going to get there?"

"Get a ride," Toby said. He was out the door.

"How are you getting back?" Bland asked.

"Get a ride," Toby said. He shut the door behind him.

Toby crossed the road in front of Raymond's and walked along the flat at the top of the hill. On his right was the Singletrees' empty house. Singletree's was the last house in the village on that side. The house was for sale. On the opposite side of the road, the tree line, and beyond the trees a night pasture where Toby could make out cows in the dark. They would have been Singletree's cows when Toby was little. Now he didn't know whose they were. He didn't pay any attention to the old farming life.

Back along the road behind Toby a car came over the hill. Its lights stretched before him. Toby turned to face the lights and held out his thumb. The car went by. For a minute Toby couldn't see. He walked along about blind. More lights hit him, and again he turned. The second car slowed, went past Toby, then ran onto the shoulder on his side and stopped. Toby hurried up to the car, opened the door.

"Evening," the driver said. Toby saw it was Mr. Crupper. He got in and shut the door. Crupper's car was dirty. It stank of gas and oil, and there was enough dirt on the floor to make another road. Toby rolled down the window on his side.

"Just get done?" Crupper asked.

"Just now," Toby said. They got back into the road, and Crupper shifted the old car and got it on its way again.

"Your boss ever going to sell that Jeep he's got outside there?" Crupper asked.

"Nobody wants it," Toby said.

"Not for a thousand dollars, anyway," Crupper said. "It doesn't look like anybody would want it."

They came to the bends, where the road went down to cross the river through a half-mile of sharp curves. Not a good place. There had been head-ons in the bends. You couldn't see. On the left was a clay bank, and on the other side, woods. Big trees stood right up to the road. Each of them had been crashed into fifty times. Their trunks on the road side were ominously cut up.

"Think he'd take seven hundred?" Crupper asked.

"No," Toby said.

"No, I don't guess he would, at that," Crupper said.

Past the bends they were out of the woods, and they went over the river in open country. Ahead were the houses and the little store at North Ambrose.

"I can get down anywhere up here," Toby said.

"You going to see the Pinto girl?" asked Crupper.

"Yes," Toby said.

"That's Rowena, isn't it? Is she the younger one? Or, no, it's a brother she's got," Crupper said.

"That's right," Toby said.

"Is she your girl now? Rowena Pinto?" Crupper asked.

"I don't know," Toby said.

"Don't know?" Crupper said. He laughed. "Yeah, well, you look out, now, if you don't know."

Rowena's was two houses past the store.

"We'll drop you right there," Crupper said, but Woody's truck was parked by the road in front of Rowena's house, and Crupper was so pleased with his joke that he forgot to slow down until he had overshot the house. Toby got out up the road.

" 'Night," Toby said to Crupper.

Crupper still thought something was funny. "Well, if you don't know, you'd best find out," he said from the driver's seat. He leaned across the seat toward the window so he could go on talking after Toby got out of the car. "If you don't know, she does. The little girl does, you can bet on that," he said.

"I guess," Toby said. He closed the door. The

door wouldn't stay. It banged shut but sprang back open. Toby closed it again. It sprang back again.

"Lift it. You got to lift it," said Crupper from inside. Toby raised the door and held onto it while he swung it shut. It stayed.

Toby walked in the dark beside Rowena's house to the rear. There was light in the kitchen. Through the window he could see Rowena at the sink. Her older brother, Woody, sat at the kitchen table. He was reading the paper.

Toby went up the step onto the little wooden porch outside. He made some noise with his feet among the pieces of firewood and plant pots stored there. He shoved the door open and went in.

"Here it comes," Rowena's brother said when Toby came in. Rowena gave him a smile from the sink. She had her arms in dishwater.

"Hi," Rowena said.

Toby sat in a chair across the table from Woody. He tilted the chair back against the wall.

"How's this?" asked Woody. He still had the paper. He read: " 'Seventy-eight LeSabre. Sixty thousand. Some rust. Engine good. New tires. Seven fifty.' What do you think?"

"Dog food," Toby said. "Take it out back. Shoot it."

"Better take the tires off first, though, don't you think?" Woody said. "Tires are new."

"I don't care," Toby said.

"Okay, now," Woody said. " 'Eighty-one LTD. Needs exhaust. Needs brake work. Body good. Texas car. Vermont inspected. One thousand or b.o.' "

"Five hundred," Toby said. "Why's he selling it?"

"Doesn't say," Woody said. "Must be his dog died. Not a big dog. A little dog, you know? Used to ride everywhere in the rear seat? Died, though. Too many memories, so he decided to sell."

"Can't ride it, can't team it, can't drive it," Toby said. "Don't make somebody else's mistake."

Rowena let the water out of the sink and sat with Toby and Woody at the table. She dried her hands on a towel. She pulled her chair beside Toby's and touched his leg under the table.

"Do you want a bottle of beer?" Woody asked.

"Oh, sure," Toby said. Rowena kissed his ear.

"You're late," she said.

"Bland was late," Toby said.

"Oh, Bland," Rowena said.

"So, uh, do you want to get the beer, there, Rowena?" Woody asked. Rowena got up and got two beers from the refrigerator. Toby opened his and handed it to Rowena. Rowena drank a little and handed the beer back.

"Where's your dad?" Toby asked.

"At school," Rowena said.

"What's up there now?" Toby asked.

"I don't know," Rowena said. "Teachers getting together. Something. He was sick two days last week. He's real tired."

"He's fine," Woody said. "How's this? 'Seventy-one Mustang. Needs clutch. Rebuilt engine. Classic. Two hundred.' "

"Glue factory," Toby said. "Put it out of its misery."

"He's not," said Rowena.

"I said he was," Woody said. Woody had hair that

was white blond, and one of his eyes pointed off at nothing. He looked at Rowena for a minute, then at Toby.

"Do you work Saturday?" he asked Toby.

"No," Toby said. "That's opening day."

"Oh, sure it is," Woody said. "Deer season. I forgot. Because, see, there's a job in Brattleboro, and I need somebody on the truck."

"Well," Toby said. "I couldn't, because of opening day."

Toby handed his beer to Rowena, but she shook her head. When Rowena was little she'd had a pony she kept in a shed behind their house. Now she worked at the hospital, in the kitchen. Her brother drove her there and back. They kept firewood in the pony's old shed. Rowena loved animals.

"Where do you go for deer?" Woody asked.

"Different places," Toby said.

"But, I mean, you go around here?" Woody asked.

"Oh, yes," Toby said.

"Well, do you sleep out there, camp, or what?" Woody asked.

"No," Toby said. "Camping's for campers, my dad says. We get up early, though."

"You can't kill anything just camping," Rowena said. "So it's no fun."

Rowena had straight hair that was almost as light blond as Woody's. It hung down her back nearly to her waist. She took a strand of her hair in her fingers, looked closely at it, and put it back behind her shoulder. She took up another strand.

"Isn't that right?" Rowena asked.

Toby didn't say anything. He had hunted deer each fall since he was eleven.

"What does it do for you, to kill a deer?" Rowena asked.

"I wouldn't know," Toby said. "I never killed one yet."

"I just don't see why it's fun. It can't be fun," Rowena said.

"Not for the deer, I guess," Toby said.

"Ah, sure it is," Woody said. "They like it when it stops, you know?"

A car stopped outside the house. In the kitchen they could hear its big engine from the road. Toby got up and went to the window to look, but he couldn't see the road. There was the sound of a footstep on the porch outside the kitchen, and somebody rapped on the door, not with a hand, but with something hard like a ring or a key. Rowena left her chair and went to the door. Toby sat down again. Rowena stood in the door with her back to the room.

"Yes?" she said.

"Johnson," a man's voice said from outside. "I'm looking for the Johnsons. Would they be anybody you know?"

"No," Rowena said. "I don't know any Johnsons here."

"Is this Newfane?" the man asked.

"No," Rowena said. "This is Ambrose. Newfane's ten or fifteen miles back."

"Right," the man outside said. "So am I headed right for Newfane, or what?"

"No," Rowena said. "Go left out of here. Bear left, then left again."

"Okay," the man said. "Left, then left again. Fifteen miles. I've got that. I'm obliged."

"Good night," said Rowena. She shut the door.

In a moment they heard the car's engine in the road again, a deep, low stirring. Woody was at the window.

"What is it?" Toby asked him.

"Can't see," Woody said. "It's wicked big, though, by the sound."

Rowena had gone to the stove and turned the flame on under the teakettle.

"Who was he?" Woody asked her. He went back to the table and sat down.

"Nobody," Rowena said.

"Well," said Woody. "What did he look like?"

"Nothing," Rowena said.

"Did you see the car?" Woody asked.

"No," Rowena said.

"He was dressed up," she said after a minute.

"Must be it's the Pork that went up earlier," Toby said.

Rowena made a cup of coffee at the stove, but rather than take it to the table and sit with Toby and Woody, she stood at the stove and drank her coffee there. From his chair Woody looked over at her.

"So?" he said. "What?"

"What?" Rowena said.

"You're a real bitch princess, aren't you, Rowena?" Woody said.

"No," Rowena said.

"Your friend's here, you know that?" Woody asked.

"I know," Rowena said.

Woody picked up the paper and shook it out on the table in front of him.

" 'Porsche,' " he read. " 'Eighty-six. No miles. No rust. Never driven. Perfect. Needs nothing. For giving away free to a really nice guy.' "

"Sure," Toby said. Rowena drank her coffee at the stove and looked toward the kitchen window, but you couldn't see through it because it was dark.

" '. . . For giving away to a deer hunter,' " Woody read.

"No kidding," Toby said. At the stove Rowena held her coffee cup between her two hands as though she were standing naked beside a campfire out in the cold woods.

" '. . . For giving away to a gas-station attendant,' " Woody read.

Woody laid the paper on the floor beside his chair. He picked up his bottle of beer, but it was empty. He shook the can and put it back on the table.

"So," he said. "Do you guys want me to go upstairs and watch TV? Want me to take a drive? Anything like that?"

"I've got to go," Toby said.

"No, you don't. Come on," Woody said. "I could just go to bed. Whatever."

"No," Toby said. He went to the door. "See you," he said.

"How are you going to get back?" Woody asked.

"Get a ride," Toby said.

★ ★ ★

Outside Toby crossed the road and started walking through the village. None of the houses except Rowena's showed a light. Toby's footsteps on the gravel beside the road were loud. At one of the houses a dog heard them and barked, then quit. Past the houses the road was straight where the land lay flat between the village and the river. Toby walked in the center of the road.

He heard a car behind him before he saw its lights. He got to the side, turned. The car was coming slowly, and as it came up to Toby he could feel the steady, deep concussion of its engine, shifted down. The car stopped beside him. He bent down to look in through the passenger's-side window and saw inside the car in the lights from the dashboard an arm in some dark material with a white cuff at the wrist. The arm was reaching over to open the door.

"Newfane," Toby heard the voice in the car say. "Am I right for Newfane?"

"Yes," Toby said. "Left up the way here."

"Yeah," said the voice. "Well, a girl back there told me to go left back up where I've come from."

"No," Toby said. "This is the road. I'm going that way myself."

"Right," the voice in the car said. Toby was down on one knee in the road beside the low car. He was looking in the window at the driver, but all he could see was the driver's white shirt cuff on the hand that held the car door open, and the many faint lights on the dash.

"Why not ride?" the driver asked. "Show me the road."

"I don't mind," Toby said.

"Right," the driver said. "Get in." His arm disappeared.

Toby got in beside the driver. The door swung shut lightly behind him and closed with a single soft click. The driver put the car in gear, and Toby sat back in his seat. He looked about him at the dark interior of the car: the glowing dashboard; the switches and dials; the driver's hand resting on the short gearshift between them on the floor; the leather seats, grips, and panels. He could smell the leather.

"Like it?" Toby asked the driver.

"What's that?" the driver said.

"The car. It's all right," Toby said.

"Right," the driver said. "It's a machine."

He put it in gear, and they moved off. In a minute he shifted, and the car gained speed. Toby saw the driver's hand move easily on the stick as he got ready to shift again.

"Do you like cars?" the driver asked.

"I guess," Toby said.

"Right," the driver said. "You'll like this, then." Ahead the turn came up that went to Brattleboro.

"Here's your left," Toby said.

"Plenty of time," the driver said. He shifted up, and they blew it right past the turn and on toward the bends. Toby looked at the dials in front of the driver. Past the left to Brattleboro they were at seventy and making speed.

"I noticed a little stretch up here I thought you'd enjoy," the driver said.

Toby put his hand up on the dash to brace himself. They went into the bends never going less than sixty. Just as well old Crupper wasn't coming down the other way; but if he had been he would have been safe enough, unless he died of fright; the driver knew his car. He shifted down, up. He steered hard, let up when he had to, punched it when he could. They came out of the bends like a racetrack rabbit and cruised easily up the road toward Raymond's. Toby sat back.

"What do you think?" the driver asked.

"It's all right," Toby said.

"Beats the hell out of milking cows, wouldn't you say?"

"I don't milk cows," Toby said.

"Sure," the driver said. "Whatever."

They were at Raymond's. It was closed. The driver turned around the pumps and got ready to go back down the way they had come. Toby looked out at the station. It was locked up and dark.

They didn't get back on the road right away but remained paused by the pumps at Raymond's. The driver sighed. He rested his hands on the top of the steering wheel. Toby could see the length of his white shirt cuffs. The driver's face was in the dark.

"Well," said the driver. "Now comes the hard part."

"What's that?" Toby asked.

"I need to be in New York—in what?—five hours, a little less."

"Mostly you couldn't do it," Toby said. "With this, you might."

"No chance," said the driver. "I don't have the gas."

"Gas in Brattleboro," Toby said. "All night."

"Here it is," the driver said. "I'm out of money." He took the car out into the road again then, and they started back toward the bends, gathering speed.

"Couldn't you ask your friends in Newfane?" Toby asked the driver.

"You aren't getting it," the driver said. "I need money now. From you. Your money is what I need now."

"Well, I don't have much," Toby said.

"Some, though," the driver said. "Not much, but some. Am I right?"

"Some, yes," Toby said.

"Take it out," the driver said. "Put it on the shelf there."

"Why?" Toby said. "Why should I?"

"Come on," the driver said. "You had a good ride, a little excitement. You liked it; I could tell. You know what it costs to run this thing? You need to contribute. Plus, if you don't—contribute—I'll get us back in the course down here and I'll put us right into a tree."

"You wouldn't do it," Toby said. "You wouldn't wreck the car for gas money."

"Oh, man, man," the driver said. "What makes you think the car is important to me? What makes you think it's even mine?"

Toby didn't say anything for a minute. They went into the bends and started to run. The driver went well out on the curves, and their headlights raced across the gray trunks of the trees that grew in the woods beside the road.

"You're kidding," Toby said.

"Think so?" the driver said. "Cost you just an

awful lot to find out I'm not, wouldn't you say? And not too much to stay ignorant. That's still cheap." He fought the wheel.

Toby pulled his wallet out of his pants and tossed it onto the shelf over the dash.

"I like that," the driver said. "What have you got there, about?"

"About twenty," Toby said.

"I like that," the driver said. He reached for the wallet and took it. Coming out of the bends at the river end again, he whipped it. They went past ninety on the way back toward the turn to Brattleboro. Approaching the turn, however, the driver slowed, and when he turned off they were creeping.

"Okay, stand by," the driver said. "I'm going to stop on the wrong side of the road up here. You get out in a big hurry, and you go right over to the other side, away from the car. Move fast, or I'll pop the clutch and drag you all the way to New York. What a mess, right? Okay?"

He stopped the car.

"Go," he said.

Toby opened the door and got out. He stepped quickly across the road and turned. Inside the car the driver called out to him.

"Beautiful," he said. "It's been a real pleasure showing you around, man. When you get to the city, be sure and look me up. We okay on that?" He shut the door. He took off.

Toby had most of nine miles to go to get home. He walked down the center of the cold road late at night. No other cars came past.

The constable lived in a house near Toby's.

When he reached there it was nearly dawn. He was going to stop and wake up the constable, but he didn't. He went on home, let himself in the kitchen. Everybody was asleep. He had been up all night, and now outside it was gray. As he had walked home it had seemed clear to Toby that he would marry Rowena. He would have kids with Rowena, and they would live together in the village. He and Woody would be friends, or they wouldn't. And if Rowena didn't like him deer hunting, well, nobody had to like everything. Or maybe he'd quit.

3

Not EVERYONE Can Be a SOLDIER

That was the best time to paint, Willard said, at the turning of the year, when the hot days had taken the wet out of the walls. One day in late August, before I had to go back to school, we started.

This painting was going to be different from my father's the summer before. This was going to take time. Willard set me to scraping the old paint. My father had not done that on the side of the house he had painted last year. Willard drew his scraper over a windowsill, and the old paint came off in a dry shower.

"You might as well not paint at all if you don't scrape first," Willard said.

I heard you, Willard. The summer before, my father had painted without scraping. Now he was away at the war, and Willard was helping my mother, me, and my baby sister, Katharine, by doing things around our house that we couldn't do ourselves. For one thing,

33

Willard and I were going to make a proper job of painting the house.

"You can do it right and do it once," said Willard. "Or you can do it quick and do it over."

Not that my father would have done that job any way but quick, even if he had been around. He was not susceptible to Willard Kent's high-minded notions of how to paint a house. They were a part of Vermont, and Vermont bored my father to death. When he was with us there, before he went overseas, all he did was tap his foot and drum his fingers. He was waiting for the war.

Let me tell you about the war: the good war, I mean, the big one, Number Two. The war had a secret, and you don't understand anything unless you know it. The secret was this: it was fun. For a few years the great machine of history became visible, and millions of ordinary men and women were required to make it run and to look on. That same machine could grind you among its fearful wheels; it could take your life. But if you were lucky, if you stayed clear, nothing could be more exciting. If you had never been anywhere, you could travel; if you were bored, here was a great effort; if nothing had ever happened in your life, here was the whole world on fire. The war was your ticket.

My father joined the Army as soon as he could find a fancy job. He was not going to go in as cannon fodder. He wound up as a press officer on the allied headquarters staff, and in the late summer of 1943 he went to England, I suppose to have some part in preparing for the invasion the next spring. Essentially, he never came back. After the war my father and mother never quite got back together again. Just like Germany.

We had been living in New York before the war. When my father joined the army, he and my mother gave up their apartment there, and my mother took my sister, who was then newborn, and me to live in her grandparents' old house in Ambrose, Vermont, north of Brattleboro. For her it was going home. She had grown up in that country, spent her summers in that house. We lived in Ambrose from about Christmas 1942. My father was with us there off and on before he went overseas. He came and went that summer.

We lived in a white house a mile and a half from Ambrose village. My mother is still there. I'm on the next hill. My father is back in New York. He has a new place, a little flat on east Ninety-second Street. He still goes downtown, but not every day. A woman comes in to keep the place straightened. I stay there with my father sometimes; he has a spare bedroom full of books. He has seen no reason to leave off his mockery of Vermont. A couple of years ago I took a job teaching at a school in one of the towns near Ambrose.

"Teaching what?" my father asked.

"English," I said.

"Oh?" my father said. "When did they start talking English up there?"

Forty years ago my father was a small, handsome man who was wise to everything. In Ambrose he sat out on the grass beside our house in a canvas chair with a week's worth of city newspapers lying on the grass beside him. He's reading the war news. I can see him. His hair is cut short. Did he want to look younger than he was, to look like a soldier? It's a hot day, and my father has taken off his shirt. On his chest and shoulders he has no more hair than I. He says, "I thought I heard the noon whistle. Who will bring me a gin and tonic? Will you bring me one, Rob?"

★ ★ ★

I was in school in New Hampshire, not too far from home, if you could make the trip; but my mother didn't let me come home except during the big vacations, and so when I got off the train in Brattleboro on a day in early June 1944, I hadn't been home since Christmas. My father was in England. I was going home to spend the summer with my mother and little sister at the house in Ambrose.

Willard Kent had his truck at the station to meet me. My mother hadn't come. It wasn't as if I didn't know Willard Kent. He had the farm next to our property in Ambrose. When we needed a hand for any simple thing, Willard was around. Years later I learned that Willard and my mother were in fact cousins, though remotely.

Willard wasn't in the war. I can remember standing with him in the dark interior of the town garage in Ambrose. Arthur Tavistock, who ran the garage then, asked, "Do you wish you were in it, Will?" And Willard seemed to think for a minute and then said, "I guess not." He was too old for the army, and something was the matter with his heart. In Ambrose, Kent boys were said to be not strong.

Willard was tall and thin, and he had an enormous angular nose that sloped elegantly down from his eyes and dropped off sharply like a stone ledge. He would have made a beautiful butler except for his smell, which was of farm animals, wood smoke, kerosene, and wet wool. It was his smell mainly that made me not happy to ride beside Willard in his truck back to Ambrose. I opened the window.

"You warm?" Willard asked.

"Yes. Hot," I said.

"Why don't you take your coat off, then?" Willard said.

I don't remember that we spoke again on the drive. No thirteen-year-old kid who is any good can make polite conversation, and Willard himself was just as happy to shut up.

At our house we found my mother standing before the long flower bed that ran under the windows at one side of the building. Willard stopped the truck, and I got out and went over to my mother.

"I was trying to decide what to do about the flowers," she said when I came up beside her.

"What did you decide?" I asked.

"Just grass would be a lot less work," my mother said. She turned to me and took my face between her hands and gave me a big kiss on the mouth. That was embarrassing, but Willard Kent had missed it. He was carrying my suitcase into the house.

"I'm glad you're here," my mother said to me. "There's so much to do."

"I'm on vacation," I said.

"Hah," my mother said. "Vacation is where you've been."

I had to help my mother to her seat. She had twisted her ankle. She sat out in front of the house on a long chair. Now I sat beside her on the edge of the chair, and for a moment she smoothed my hair with her fingers, patted my shoulder, held my hand. As always, I smelled smoke. When she had kissed me a moment earlier her lips had tasted of tobacco, and I saw in the grass under her chair a cigarette end with lipstick on it. My mother smoked them by the pack. All the women I remember from that time smoked. Not all the men did. My father, for example, never smoked. Willard Kent didn't smoke. But the women smoked and left red cigarette ends here and there—woman's unmistakable trace.

"You're right," my mother says today. "We all smoked like chimneys. Well, what if we did?"

My mother does better today as an old lady than she did as a war wife. She must be happier. She is a kind of character in town, I think. The younger people like her. She's filled out a bit. Then she was skinny. In 1944 she was thirty-five. She had: no husband, a silent son, an infant daughter, relatives, no friends, an old car, a house, enough money. Very well, she would manage. Others, with less, managed. It was a question of taking care of things until the kids were in bed each night.

"Sit down and let me look at you," my mother said. I sat down and let her look at me. She looked for a sign that something had at last come along at school to make me different from and better than what I had been. I let her see that nothing had.

How did I fill the days? I have no idea. Maybe that was the summer I learned to read like a grownup— or like a kid: sitting in the warm grass with his nose in a book while about him the air buzzes, and the trees hum, and overhead the blue sky passes, and he knows nothing about any of it. I had discovered the English subclassics, and all day I read *A Study in Scarlet, The Adventures of Sherlock Holmes,* and other stories of the famous detective. I read lying on my stomach in the green grass beside our house, killing mosquitoes and letting little bugs crawl over the pages.

My mother walked painfully on her injured ankle. Willard Kent was around. He knew how to keep a place up: our place and his own both were not too much for him. I looked out the window and saw Willard cutting the grass beside the house. His head moved back and forth across the window. My mother had done that job.

"He's cutting the grass," I said to my mother. "You cut the grass."

"Not any more," my mother said.

Mr. Holmes, it was the footprint of a gigantic hound.

Willard Kent was digging the garden. Always my mother had tied a handkerchief around her hair and put on strong shoes; then she had jumped on the garden fork with both feet while I waited to pull the biggest stones out of the earth and roll them away. Now Willard Kent dug slowly.

He sets the fork, places his right foot on it, and shoves it easily into the ground, then brings it up, jogs it, and moves along. When he hits a big stone he goes around it; he knows a few stones in a garden do no harm. Later he'll come back with a rake and a hoe and bust the clods and smooth the ground for planting. Willard does it all. "She ought not to do that," he says. Is that because she has hurt her ankle?

"Go see if you can't be a help to Mr. Kent sometimes," my mother told me.

"A help with what?" I asked.

"Well, I don't know, ask him. With whatever he

needs help with," she said. In a minute she was going to start looking at me.

"I don't think he needs any help," I said.

"Just go see next time he's around, would you?" my mother said. "Just ask him? It's not as though you had anything better to do. I'd think you'd want to do something. You must be bored."

"No," I said. "I like not doing anything."

"Come on, Rob, don't be a jerk," my mother said. "You have to, that's all."

I was being a jerk, but I was right. Willard didn't need my help. He had it anyway, though. A section of the fence that kept Willard's cows out of the woods on the hill behind our house sagged badly. I was to help Willard fix it. We took a spool of barbed wire, a posthole digger, wire cutters, the axe, a hammer, nails, fence staples, and the fence-puller. Willard had the stuff in his truck, and we bumped up the pasture beside the cool woods with the sun in the pasture on our right hand and the woods green and dark on our left.

We found that one of the posts in the weak section of fence was pulled over to one side. Willard cut the wire close to the post, worked the post up out of the ground, and set to improving its hole with the posthole digger. He told me to cut out the rest of the wire in the weak section. "We ought to put in new wire all along," Willard said.

Willard set the post back in its hole. Then he went into the woods with the axe and cut a stout sapling. He cut off the bottom to make a section about eight feet long and made a point at one end. He propped the sapling against the weak post, forcing the post to stand upright, and put two big nails through the end of the sapling into the post.

"Post ought to have been braced when it was set," Willard said.

Willard stapled one end of the new wire to the braced post and gave me the spool to carry down the fence to the next post. I suppose it was fifteen feet away. I had the fence-puller, a lever mounted to pivot on a steel claw, which you clamped on a fence post to stretch wire tight before you stapled it down onto the post. Willard told me to fix my end of the wire onto the puller and hook it on the next post, which was firm. I did. Willard told me to pull the lever around to tighten up the wire. We had too much wire out, and the puller worked easily but didn't stretch the wire. I hitched the wire up tight and tried the puller again. Now I couldn't move it. It was too hard. I threw my weight back to pull the lever around, but I couldn't make it come.

Willard came down the fence. He took hold of the lever and pulled. He stopped, set his feet, and pulled again. The lever went around, and the wire came up tight. Willard stapled it to the post.

"Works stiff," he said.

★ ★ ★

The summer before, waiting for the war, my father was restless. He was like a traveler who expects his train to be called: he wouldn't be long, no sense in starting anything. He climbed into our car and drove for hours among the little towns and along the brooks over the back roads. In some ways he knew that country very well.

Often I went with him. We had no adventures together, but once we stopped along a road in the middle of the woods to help a young woman whose car

had broken down. That was the summer before my
father went to England. He says he no longer remembers
our picking up the girl in the woods.

We had been driving since after breakfast. We
were coming into Black River Mills by the back way that
goes for several miles in there, between high banks
through a big woods. We passed a car pulled over, and
half a mile farther along we overtook a woman walking
down the middle of the road. When she heard our car,
she moved over to the side of the road and turned to
face us. My father stopped the car beside her. The
woman was on his side of the road.

"Lord, finally," she said. "Do you guys know
you're the only thing that's come down this road in two
hours? How about a lift?"

"You took the words out of my mouth," my
father said.

At this the woman laughed delightedly. She bent
down to look into our car. To me she said, "Hi, good
looking." She went around the front of the car and got in
beside me.

"Move over, Rob, and give the lady some room,"
my father said. I moved closer to him on the seat. The
girl got in beside me. She slammed the door. Sitting back
in the seat, she sighed.

"Oh, boy," she said. "That's better. Thanks a lot,
no kidding."

"We'll go back and try to get your car started,"
my father said.

"Can't," the girl said. "Out of gas." My father put
the car in gear, and we went on toward Black River
Mills.

"We can get gas up here a little ways," my father

said. "Then we'll bring you back out to your car, and you'll be all set."

"Oh, well, listen, no," the girl said. "This kid isn't lost, you know. But thanks. The Mills is where I'm actually going. My aunt. I'm visiting her. She can drive me back. But thanks. I really thought I was going to have to walk all the way. To my aunt's."

"It's only another mile or so," my father said.

"Yeah, well, that's what I mean. I'm pooped already," the girl said.

"Move *over*, could you, good-looking?" she said to me. I slid along closer to my father.

"You don't live in the Mills, then?" my father asked her.

"Lord, no," said the girl. "I live in Worcester, Massachusetts. I and my girlfriend have an apartment. We're bachelor girls," she laughed. "Since our husbands are away. We're married to brothers. I mean, my girlfriend's husband and my husband are brothers."

"I think I follow you," my father said. "Your girlfriend is your sister-in-law."

"Yeah, well. No, well. I don't know," the girl said.

"Well," my father said. "Her husband's your brother-in-law, right?"

"Yeah," the girl said.

"So?" my father said.

"Yeah, I guess so," the girl said.

"Where are they?" my father asked.

"Navy," the girl said. "They're both on aircraft carriers. Playing boats and planes. *Vrrrooom.*" She laughed. "'Little boys like boats and planes,' my girlfriend and I say. What are we supposed to do while they're off playing?" She pulled her dress up a little over her knees to cool her legs.

"They're not on the same ship," she went on. "They won't put you on the same ship with your brother, because if they sink it, there goes the family. Mine's at sea. I think. I'm not supposed to know. Hope you're not a spy." She opened her handbag and took out a package of cigarettes. "Is it okay?" she asked.

My father nodded. "You play, too," he said.

The girl was lighting her cigarette. "Excuse me?" she said.

"You play, too," my father said. "If your husbands are playing, you can, too. Can't you?"

"With who?" the girl said. "There isn't anybody."

She spoke to me: "You're not a spy, are you, good-looking?" she asked.

I like to died.

"You're the strong, silent type, I guess," the girl said. "I think that's real attractive. So many men nowadays think they can talk a girl right into—well, anything." She laughed, blew out smoke.

"What's your aunt's name?" my father asked the girl. "I know some people in the Mills."

"Mrs. Garibaldi," the girl said. "I bet you don't know her."

"You're right," my father said. He grinned. Again the girl laughed as at a good, old joke. We were coming into Black River Mills. It's not a big place: fifteen houses, a store. My father stopped the car. The girl climbed out.

"This is great. Thanks a million, really. And so long, Gary Cooper," the girl said. She waved her fingers in the car window, turned, and began walking up a short lane that ran back from the road toward the hillside.

There were three or four houses on it. She looked back once, waved again, walked on. My father watched her back. I watched her back.

"I wonder which is her aunt's," I said.

My father snorted. "What aunt?" he said.

"What?" I said.

My father said nothing. He pulled the car into the road, and we moved off. "And she's got a husband on an aircraft carrier?" he said. "She and her girlfriend and her aunt? Mrs. Garibaldi, her aunt?" He shook his head and grinned.

"War is hell," my father said.

★ ★ ★

When Willard Kent and I painted the house, we did the south side only. Our house got painted in the old New England country way, one side each year, going around. It was the east side that my father had done the summer before. This year Willard and I were to do the south side. Our house was white, and its window shutters were black. Even the houses up there look like cows, my father used to say.

We took a day to scrape the wall. Then we did it all again with wire brushes. Then we went over the wall with hammers and pounded down loose clapboard nails. Then we puttied cracks. Then we painted.

The summer before, my father had painted carelessly. I can see him slapping it on. He's wearing old brown pants and a white T-shirt that is very clean. Some white paint spots are on the skin of his arms, one is in his hair. Probably he has some spots on his T-shirt, too, but you can't tell because it's white like the paint. He is throwing the paint on fast, working hard, speckling the grass, the flowers, himself. And as I will learn the next year, he's got it backwards. He's painting up; he should be painting down. Did he not know how to do it right, or did he know and not care?

Now Willard Kent and I began by painting the shutters. We had taken them off the house and propped them against one another on the grass. When the shutters were done we set our ladders on either side of the house's end and started on the house itself. The new white paint spread down over the house, ahead of the morning light. I tried to draw my brush firmly along, as Willard did his.

I had never known how complex a thing the outside of a house is, a simple clapboard wall. You couldn't attend to it in a hurry, as my father had either believed or pretended. Scraping the old paint off, then putting on fresh, on the ground and up on my ladder, I learned of the thousand cracks and holes in the wall; its nails, pins, and patches; its inhabitants: mice, spiders, beetles, wasps.

Willard smashed a wasp against the house with his fist.

"What is it?" I asked him.

"Another bee," Willard said. Any flying insect that looked as if it would sting, he called a bee.

It took us longer to paint our side of the house than it had taken my father to paint his, but not a lot longer. When we finished, my mother was out on the grass looking with us up at the wall and at our ladders standing high against it. The sun shining on the new white paint hurt your eyes.

Willard went home for lunch. He was going to

come back later to replace the shutters, supposing they were dry. I was in the house upstairs, where Sherlock Holmes, his case concluded, was once again about to bring together for his happy reader the parts of the late problem, fixing them at last, demonstrating method, motive, and identity. I read on. My father was in Paris. The war was supposed to be about over. We had had letters from my father when he had been in London. Yes, he wrote faithfully. He wrote about the buzz bombs, and he wrote that General Patton was a lunatic and that the British were finished.

In early August my father went across to France, and at the end of the month, around the time Willard and I began to paint the house, he wrote that Paris had been liberated by two Jeeps in which rode a private in the Signal Corps who had gotten lost, a lady photographer who was drunk, Ernest Hemingway, and seven correspondents from the Chicago *Tribune.*

Reading in my room, I heard something hit the ground outside, and then something heavier right behind it. My mother was going down the stairs fast, and then she was running out of the house. Running. In her room upstairs, where my mother had been with her, my sister began to cry. I ran downstairs.

Outside I saw one of the window shutters lying on the grass at a distance from the house. I came around the side of the house and felt my heart turn over when I saw Willard. He lay on his back beside the foundation. He couldn't move. Bright blood ran out of his hair, down his forehead, and into his ear where it pooled, overflowed, and dripped quickly away into the grass. My mother knelt at Willard's chest, and I saw her hands were on him, touching his chest, his hands, his forehead, comforting him. I came up to them. Willard's eyes were open. He was conscious. He was looking around him, looking up at my mother. All the color had left him, and his face was white.

"Go upstairs to the big chest," my mother said. "Get all the blankets you can carry and bring them down here. Bring a towel for the blood. Put the blankets around him, but don't try to tuck them under him or make him move. He mustn't move. Stay with him. I'll go for help. I'll get somebody. I'll take the baby with me. Hurry, now." She laid her hand on Willard's chest and said to him, "I'll be quick."

I got the blankets. As I was going downstairs with them, I became afraid I would find Willard dead. What would I do then? I would cover him up. I heard our car start. My mother was going. Outside, around the house, Willard wasn't dead. He opened his mouth when I got down by him with my blankets, but still he couldn't speak. He looked at me. He cleared his throat.

"Got that towel?" he said.

I had it in my hand. I gave it to Willard. Slowly he raised his hand and mopped the blood from his face with the towel. He held the towel to his head.

"Came off the ladder," Willard said. "Good thing I landed on my head. Might have hurt myself."

I began to lay the blankets over Willard as my mother had told me to, but he said, "I don't want them." Then Willard said, "Your father is a fine man. He'll be home soon. They all will. They have about won. He is safe. He is a fine, smart man, your father."

Willard was all right. He had been up near the top of his ladder, replacing the shutters on the attic window. A bee had come out of the wall and stung him on his upper lip. Willard had thrown the shutter away and tipped the ladder over. It was a twenty-foot fall, but he landed flat out on grass. He bumped his head and cracked two ribs. They sewed up his head and taped his ribs, and by the time I went back to school he was putting on the rest of the shutters.

★ ★ ★

For a long time I used to go to bed early. There I read my many books. Mr. Holmes, it was the footprint of a gigantic hound. Mr. Holmes, these stories have been about memory, what it tells you and what it doesn't, what you have to figure out. They don't always overlap. There are true memories, and there are new memories, but there are no true, new memories. In my life people were falling from great heights, or they were driving around assisting females of doubtful modesty, or they were or were not conducting obscure courtships with honest peasants. And all that time history was going on around them, so close. But history is not memory. You have to learn it.

Let me tell you about the war.

4

That Is No COUNTRY for Old MEN

Huey still rolled his own. He was rolling one now with his aged fingers, while Johnson's new hand, whose name was Erskine, walked around the carcass of Gentleman Jack, the horse, looking for a piece of ground he could get his spade into. Huey didn't know whether Erskine was the hand's first name or his last name. Most of the hired men were the same: no names, no addresses, no good ends.

"*Erskine,*" Huey said. "What kind of a name is that? That an Irish name?"

"I don't know," Erskine said. He poked Jack's side with the toe of his boot.

"You ought to know," Huey said. "It's your name, isn't it? Maybe it's your first name. Erskine what?"

"What do you care?"

"I don't care. It's just as you like. I'm only making conversation. Just making the time pass. Is Erskine your first name?"

"Maybe."

" 'Maybe'," Huey said. "Maybe it's your last name, maybe it's your first name. Maybe it's both. Erskine Erskine. That's a hell of a name. Is that it?"

"Maybe," Erskine said.

"That's how it is with you, is it?" Huey said. "A mystery. A man who makes a mystery about his name has a reason. You are in trouble, is that it?"

"No."

"I don't see why you should worry about me," Huey said. "I couldn't do much to you."

"That's a fact," Erskine said.

Huey had an unusual way of making them. Instead of rolling the tobacco up in the paper to make the cigarette, he made the cigarette first and added the tobacco when the cigarette was finished. He rolled the paper into a tube around his forefinger. Then he licked the paper and sealed the tube. He pinched one end closed. Holding the tube upright by the closed end, he poured tobacco into the open end. The tube filled. When the cigarette was full, Huey tapped at it to settle the tobacco and poured in some more. Then he pinched the open end, and he was done.

Sometimes Huey never lit his cigarette but simply held it in his mouth, drawing on it with his lips. In time the cigarette disappeared, some of the tobacco having fallen down over Huey's front, and Huey having seemingly eaten the rest, including the paper.

Today he sat on the end of their truck and smoked. He watched Erskine circling Gentleman Jack. Erskine was nineteen or twenty. The job he had been given that day was not to his liking. Being stuck with

Huey was not to his liking. He bashed Jack's flank with his spade. He kicked him in the belly.

"Smell it?" he said.

Gentleman Jack was a draft horse of Johnson's that had died in the night and now lay at one end of an uphill pasture. Johnson told Erskine to go and bury him where he lay. Johnson didn't think Erskine was good for much. He was thinking of sending Erskine on his way. A long day's digging dirt and wrestling with a ton of Gentleman Jack's immovable carcass would do to make Erskine crave the road. Johnson didn't like to fire them; he liked them to quit on him.

Johnson told Erskine to take Huey along because it was going to be a warm day with plenty of sun. Huey was more than ninety years old. The sun kept him alive.

Erskine thought Johnson was crazy. Johnson liked to listen to himself talking. He enjoyed the sound of his voice forming words, sentences, expressing his mind.

"Do you know how to bury a horse?" Johnson had asked him.

"Sure," Erskine said.

"How are you going to do it, then?"

"How do you bury anything?" Erskine said. "You dig a hole. Then you put it in the hole. Then you fill the hole up."

"You are quite a man," Johnson said. "You are able to pick up a dead horse and toss it into a hole."

"All right, how do you want me to do it?" Erskine asked him.

"You have to get right next to the body and dig under and around it. You are digging the dirt out from under it, so it sinks down. You don't really bury it, you see—well, you do, but the way you do it is you turn it under. Or you turn what's under it over. Depends on how you look at it. It's up to you."

"All right," Erskine said.

"You can bury anything that way," Johnson went on. "There was a man around here years ago—Huey probably remembers him—he buried a whole pig house that way, just turned it inside out. It wasn't a little pig house, either, was it, Huey? Remember him, do you?"

"That's right," Huey said.

"I'll tell you," Johnson said. "One thing: You really get to know that horse. You get right next to it, as I said. You're loving that horse. You can taste it. If the horse has bugs, you get bugs, and if you have bugs, the horse gets bugs."

"The difference is that it doesn't matter to the horse—having bugs," Huey said.

"Right," Erskine said.

"There is that difference," Johnson said. "Anyway, you really get to know that horse."

The big horses at Johnson's had been famous. Gentleman Jack was the last of them. They didn't live forever. While they lived, though, they could pull almost anything, because they were bigger than almost anything.

He lay out on his right side. His legs, together, stretched before him, and his belly and flanks thrust up in a great hump. In his open mouth the big teeth were visible.

Erskine wasn't getting anywhere with him. Trying to bury Jack by digging away the earth from around him, Erskine saw, he would need to dig up three-quarters of the pasture to get him underground. He wasn't setting about it in the right way. Intolerably, it seemed you had to plan and ponder even to put a dead horse under the grass. Even in a thing like that you couldn't just walk up to it and do it.

"Get in," Erskine said to Huey. "We're going back."

"What for?"

"To get some boards."

"He's laughing at you," Huey said.

★ ★ ★

Erskine drove the truck into the yard before the house Huey lived in. They kept a stack of lumber out back. When Erskine and Huey drove into the yard, a kid who was playing at the side stopped what she was doing and ran up onto the porch and into the house. Erskine got down from the truck. A radio began to play inside the house. Huey stayed in the truck. Erskine went across the yard toward the house. He was about to climb the step onto the porch when the door opened. Johnson stepped out of the house onto the porch. The radio was playing loudly.

"What are you doing here?" Johnson said. "Where's Huey?"

Inside the radio was still playing. "I can't hear you," Erskine said. The radio's noise quieted, then stopped altogether.

"Where's Huey?" Johnson said again.

"In the truck."

"What do you mean, in the truck?" Johnson said. He looked across the yard.

"I mean he's sitting in the truck. What do you want from me?"

Johnson looked again and saw in the yard the truck and Huey sitting in it.

"What did you come back for?" he asked.

"I need some boards," Erskine said. "And I need a saw."

"What do you need that for?" Johnson asked him.

"Get under him. Or something—so I can dig."

Johnson looked at Erskine.

"The horse," Erskine said. "The horse I'm burying."

Johnson looked at him a little longer. "Take what you need," he said. Then he came down off the porch and walked past Erskine and on out of the yard.

Erskine got four long timbers and carried them out to the truck. He got a saw and threw it in after the timbers. Then he climbed up into the driver's seat, and he and Huey drove back to the pasture where Gentleman Jack lay. Erskine drew the truck alongside Jack. He got out and went around to the back of the truck. He got up onto the back and threw the four timbers and the saw down beside Jack. Then he jumped down himself and set to work. Huey got down from his seat. He stood in the grass beside the truck and watched. Erskine started shoving one of the timbers under Jack's forequarters.

Huey looked up at the sun, then around for a place to sit. He sat down in the grass with his back against one of the truck's front wheels. Huey tilted his head back and let the sun hit his throat and breast. The sun beat upon him. He heard Erskine strike his spade into the sod before Jack's head, and he heard the sod tear free when Erskine worked his spade beneath it.

Huey couldn't get enough of the sun. He wished sometimes he could slit himself open right from the chin to the crotch. He would lay back the flesh and let the sun into the dark insides; it would quicken them. Nothing could be worse than burial. Don't you bury me, but just roll me out into the yard and turn me over on my back.

Erskine climbed out of the ground. He had started running a deep trench under Gentleman Jack, whose carcass rested above the pit on the timbers Erskine had shoved under him. Erskine removed his shirt. He had been working in the hole for a long time, and he was bent over; he wanted to come loose as he always did. He reached his arms up above his head and arched his body backward from the waist, reaching for the ground behind his heels. Huey looked on. Erskine straightened up and went into a little crouch. He rolled his shoulders in and out. The muscle moved across his upper back.

"Why don't you save it for the little girls," Huey said. "It's all going to waste out here."

Erskine took a comb from his pants pocket and ran it through his hair at the side. He turned to the truck and looked into the windshield, combing.

"I bet they just can't resist all those muscles, can they?" Huey said. "All that skin."

Erskine was still looking for his reflection in the windshield. "They like it," he said.

"Digging holes, that's good for the body, isn't it?" Huey said.

"Yeh," Erskine said, combing.

"Jesus," Huey said.

"What's the matter?"

"You," Huey said. "I have had to watch you all morning, and I see you have just brains enough to dig. I hope you have brains enough to walk."

"What does that mean?" Erskine asked him, but Huey had said all he had to say. Erskine got back down in his trench below Gentleman Jack and resumed digging away at it. Huey leaned his head back 'til it touched the truck tire's warm rubber, and shut his eyes. The sun burned through his eyelids.

★ ★ ★

Huey slept. He went a long way out. There was a river in his cellar.

It had rained for three days. It was raining still. The floods had started. A stream of gray water was running along a channel in the floor of the cellar. It ran from under one dripping cellar wall across the dirt floor and out under the opposite wall. He stood beside the stream and wondered what to do. The water was rising all around his house. There was no way to keep it out. He couldn't dam it, or drain it. You can't drain a stream. Shortly the stream would wash away the cellar, the foundation of his house, and the house itself would break up and be carried away. He must get out before that happened. But it didn't seem to be happening. The stream ran on through his cellar.

The water was carrying away Huey's belongings. A chair of his went bobbing by, and then some other of his personal effects. They floated past where he stood and out under the wall.

His daughter went by on the stream. She was in her bed, half undressed and kneeling among the sheets. Her underwear was down off her shoulders. God knows what she had been doing. The bed with her in it was carried by on the water.

"Whoops, whoops," Huey's daughter called to him as she went by.

"Hey," he called. *"Hey!"* But she was gone where the water went out of the cellar under the wall.

Something else of his went by. He kept on standing beside the stream in the dirt floor of his cellar. It was the worst thing that could happen to your house—a flood going right through it—and still the cellar and the house held and were not destroyed. More personal effects went by. Huey was getting bored.

"Is this how you keep up your place?"

Johnson was in the cellar with him. What was he doing there? He never came to Huey's house. What was Johnson doing down in the cellar when Huey was around?

"Is this how you keep up the place I gave you?"

Huey told him there was a flood over the whole country that was getting set to carry them all away, though nothing kept on happening. Huey's clothes tree went floating past. The clothes tree had a little wooden cup at the front for studs. Huey had never owned studs in his life. The clothes tree had been Johnson's. Johnson had given it to him.

"Is this how you keep up your place?" Johnson said again.

★ ★ ★

The sun came in through Huey's eyelids. They had parted a little. He had been asleep with his eyes open.

The sun was down over the line of trees at the end of the pasture. It struck nearly level into Huey's eyes, and seemed about to fry his eyeballs. He looked away from the sun. Erskine was standing beside Gentleman Jack. He stood with his back to Huey, his hands on his hips and his legs apart. He was pivoting his torso from side to side, facing left, then abruptly right, like a mechanical bird. He had finished digging.

Huey looked at him. "I went to sleep, I guess," he said.

"I guess so," Erskine said. "A man as old as you never knows, when he goes to sleep, does he?" he said.

"He never knows even when he wakes up again," Huey said.

"No?"

"No," Huey said. "Like right now I can't help thinking I have died and gone to hell and been sentenced to spend eternity with a no-name."

"I'm not so bad," Erskine said.

"You are," Huey said, "but why don't you try and convince me you aren't by getting that horse over with and getting us both back there."

"I still have to cover him up," Erskine said. "That will take another couple of hours."

"You can do that tomorrow," Huey said. "Right now, why not just drop him down there and then call it a day?"

"I can do that," Erskine said.

Erskine got his saw from beside the truck. He knelt by Gentleman Jack and started cutting through the timber that supported Jack's head and neck. When it was cut, the timber fell into the hole, and Jack's head and neck sagged down after it. Erskine started on the rear timber, which held Jack's hindquarters. When he had cut half the way through it, he and Huey could hear all the three timbers start to go at once. Jack's weight, which four timbers had held, was too heavy for three. Erskine pulled his saw free of the rear timber and stood back.

"She's away," Huey said.

The remaining timbers let go, and Jack dropped down. With the drop his head twisted on its neck and reared up out of that fresh brown clay.

★ ★ ★

He's laughing at you, Erskine Erskine. Oh, brother, you're smart enough to dig. But are you smart enough to walk?

5

The SONG
of ROLAND

The Weatherhead burying took place on Friday
afternoon, the day before hunting season opened. Clifford had closed the store so the people there could go
to the funeral. Roland Bailey went with the others. If
Roland hadn't gone with them to the cemetery it would
have looked as though he'd had something against Alan
Weatherhead. Well, he had.

Alan Weatherhead was no friend of Roland's.
He'd tried to steal Roland's son and turn him against his
father. He'd more than tried. Still, not everyone knew
about that, so it was easier for Roland to go to the
funeral than stay away.

At the cemetery Roland remained in the back.
By the grave were Sybil Weatherhead and her daughters,
and some others, well dressed, whom Roland didn't
know. They would be Alan Weatherhead's family or
hers. There were about twenty-five people besides, from
the town. There had been no church service; Alan

Weatherhead had not gone to church. Nevertheless, the minister read from a prayer book at his grave. That was evidently the arrangement Alan Weatherhead had wanted. He wouldn't be buried without ceremony; he wouldn't have to be, in Ambrose. He was known there. Years ago when the church that he wasn't a member of had needed a new roof, Alan Weatherhead was the one who put it on. Well, Roland Bailey and some other men put the roof on. Alan Weatherhead wrote the check.

Most people thought Alan Weatherhead high. Roland Bailey thought him so. Ambrose claimed him, nevertheless, with reservations. Alan Weatherhead was a smart man, but a modern man. One year they had asked him to give the speech on Ambrose Common at the Memorial Day parade, for he had had a naval career and then had been in Washington after the war. Alan Weatherhead agreed. Did he know he was to fail? Memorial Day in Vermont is like Christmas in Jerusalem. The organizers of the parade knew what they wanted; they knew what a Memorial Day speech was. Alan Weatherhead's speech didn't do what a Memorial Day speech had to do. He had chosen to speak hopefully of the future of the United States and of the town, of education, opportunity, and change—and not reminiscently of struggle, blood, and sacrifice. Also Alan Weatherhead hadn't wanted to join in the parade itself, and he hadn't worn his naval uniform. His speech made, he'd simply stepped down from the platform and gone home. They didn't ask him to speak again.

Roland Bailey's son, Dorman, had gone to Alan Weatherhead like a lost child, or he had at first, anyway, before he took it into his head to outrage gratitude; for

Dorr didn't suppose he belonged in Ambrose either. Alan Weatherhead welcomed him.

Alan Weatherhead could charm you. Did he know what was in Roland's mind about him? If he knew, he wouldn't have cared. Alan Weatherhead wasn't a repenter. Give him credit: he went his own way. Ambrose had housed him, and it had let him alone. That was what he had required. Now Ambrose was going to bury him.

Alan Weatherhead's grave was in a corner of the cemetery, near the stone wall. The cemetery lay on a little hill, so that Roland, in the rear, stood higher than the people closer to the grave. He couldn't hear anything that was said, so he looked over the people and into the woods that began outside the cemetery.

Behind the stone wall something red was visible. Wendell Spring, the sexton, had brought his pump up here this morning and hidden it behind the wall so it would be handy after the ceremony when he'd have to finish the grave. In November a grave would fill up with a foot of water and mud at the bottom in a few minutes, and Wendell Spring would pump it out before he lowered Alan Weatherhead and filled the hole. Wendell hated to wrestle with the pump. It was heavy and had little wheels that were meant to roll it around the floor of a factory and went badly over ground. So Wendell would haul the pump up to the cemetery beforehand when he had to use it. He'd hide it somewhere, and there it would be, peeping out from behind a tree or a big headstone at about every burying Ambrose had except those in a dry summer. After the service, when everyone had left the cemetery, Wendell would start the pump. All over the village the noise of its engine would pound away like a passing bell, and the pump would run until it had sucked all the water out of the hole, for it offended Wendell Spring to put remains down in the wet.

Roland hadn't known the ceremony had ended until he saw people nearer the grave turn and start to leave. The minister had closed his book. He was talking to the visitors. None of the women wept, none of the men. Roland left the cemetery. He walked beside the road that led down to the village. Soon cars carrying others from the funeral overtook him. They put up dust. Roland watched the dust cover his shoes while the cars passed him. Nobody offered him a ride. If anyone had, he would have said no. He hadn't far to go home. His house was on the other side of the village from the cemetery, no more than half a mile to walk—less than that from Clifford's—and the post office was on his way. He'd be stopping there.

Roland. A French knight's name, and unfit, for he was a heavy hen of a man now, with an exasperated gaze and a disposition that proclaimed he didn't need to tolerate fools or anything else at the age of—what?— sixty-six. Born on the Pied Brook road in a farmhouse that burned forty years ago; born right there, and mar- ried a Tavistock—Marjorie, the first of the five Tavistock sisters and a favorite with the older people in the town. She'd left him fifteen years ago and moved to Boston with their children, a boy and a girl, the girl the older. So Roland lived by himself in his little house above the brook that ran back of the village and worked at Clif- ford's putting up the stock, seeing to the furnace, keep- ing things in repair, and greeting any customer who greeted him, but not taking half the day over it.

Roland entered the post office. The building was dark as a cave inside, for the windows were inadequate. Three decades earlier the Government of the United States had bought Mrs. Mackenzie's old lot from her estate, including a good house and a stables. They tore down the house and turned the stables into a post office. It was then that the people of Ambrose knew a world war was inevitable. Today, when he entered the room, Roland paused before going to his mailbox. Someone was talking to him.

The post office was a long room with brass-fronted mailboxes making up one wall in which was also a brass window, barred. Over it a plate cast in brass said STAMPS. Opposite, a library table with an electric lamp, and on the wall above it a portrait of the president and a bundle of notices: fugitives. Roland every day half expected to see his son's photograph on one of those notices.

"Edith called up on the telephone this morning. Well, it was nearer noon."

The postmistress was talking to him from behind the wall of mailboxes. Roland couldn't see her. The postmistress was a shy soul. She was one of Perley Taft's daughters from North Ambrose, but she had dark skin, and she had one eye brown, the other blue. By the time she was grown she had been so taunted and tormented that when she came to the post office she preferred not to show herself. She stayed behind the mailboxes, coming out only to sell a stamp from the barred window, which itself hid her pretty well. Still, she liked to talk, and she would peep through the mailboxes and carry on with her women customers as though they were sitting across a kitchen table.

"She called up the store, but the line was busy, she said," the postmistress told Roland.

"What did she want?" Roland asked her.

"She wanted to know if a letter she sent had come for you," the postmistress said. "If it had, she said you're to be sure and read it before you go home."

"Has it?"

"I'm sure I don't know," the postmistress said. "I put one up for you, but I didn't notice who it was from. I don't have time to read every envelope, you know."

Roland found his mailbox, opened it. Through the box he could see the postmistress's brown eye looking at him from her dark face. That was her right eye, the brown one. There was a letter. He took it out and opened it. He shut the door of his mailbox.

"How is Edith?" the voice of the postmistress asked. "Let me see. It seems as though she's not married." This was the day the postmistress meant to get current on Roland's life, he saw, though ordinarily she hadn't much to say to men. She felt badly for having snapped at him over his letter from Edith.

"No," Roland said. "She works for some lawyers down there."

"Oh yes," the postmistress said. "And then Marjorie still lives with her, is that right?" From behind her wall where nobody could see her, the postmistress could speak of anything, any old, forbidden subject, and get a civil answer, and even a relevant one sometimes.

"No, she lives on the next street," Roland said.

He couldn't read Edith's letter in the post office, because there wasn't light enough. He started for the door. "Well, greet Edith for me if you're writing," the postmistress called after him. She and Edith were the same age.

Outside, Roland unfolded Edith's letter. Edith didn't know Alan Weatherhead was dead. He would have to write her now. Edith's letter was four sheets closely written with a typewriter, on both sides. His daughter's letters wore him out. This one he had to read before he went home. Why?

He read: Edith had met someone she'd known from Ambrose on Commonwealth Avenue. Mother twisted her ankle. She is so tired at the end of her day. A movie they saw: James Bond. Diane . . . Friday. Be nice. Dorr.

"Warm for this late?"

"It is," Roland said. Somebody had gone past him, into the post office. He read the page again.

Dorr's girl stayed with me for two nights. She hitchhiked here from Washington, D.C. Four hundred miles. She's very _nice_, no great brain, but very much in love with Dorr. (I wonder if it's mutual.) Dorr is on his way to Montreal—he has a friend there who has a job for him. (Can you go to Canada and get a job just like that—it's a foreign country, not the Good Old U.S.A.? Don't worry, I didn't ask.)

They planned it that she will go on up there and meet him next weekend. Since you're on her way (sort of) she wants to stop in Ambrose and visit—I didn't think you'd be thrilled but I didn't know how to say no (mother doesn't even know about her), and so I said she should go ahead. She expects to get there Friday (hitchhiking, so she can't say when). Be nice to her, for I'm sure it would mean a lot to Dorr (well that's not true, I don't know if she means anything to him, but be nice to her anyway). She's a good heart, just irresponsible. Very much a city kid—knows nothing but will do anything. You'll see. I talked to Dorr when she called him. He said to say hello to you. His girl's name is Diane. (Oh, I forgot to say her dog will be there, too.)

Good Lord. Today was Friday.

Was what's-her-name going to spend the night? Probably she was; she couldn't start out hitchhiking again this evening, though a girl who would hitchhike to Vermont from Washington, D.C., was obviously not a worrier. And if she didn't care what happened to her, why should he? Edith had wanted to make sure he didn't get home and just find her there. He hated surprises, and Edith knew it. She had all the brains in that family. Marjorie, too. He and Dorr were the dumb ones.

Roland crossed the road and walked out of the village toward the turn to his house. Ahead he could see his roof and chimney. Was she there now? He felt his legs taking him closer to home.

How well did what's-her-name know Dorr? Did she know how Dorr left home? Roland had been wakened in the middle of the night by a thumping and banging from the attic and, going to investigate, he'd found Dorr, drunk, trying to drag a trunk down the narrow stairs. Roland yelled at him, and Dorr dropped the trunk and came down from the attic. He wanted a fight. Roland was three-quarters asleep. Dorr wasn't making sense, and he stank of beer. Roland became angry. "You're drunk. Go to bed," he ordered Dorr, and gave him a shove. But this time Dorr shouted right back at him: "You don't tell me what to do, you bastard, you're not my father!" and brought around a wild right hand that landed on Roland's ear and knocked him through the railing and down the stairs to the first floor. When he woke up he was sitting on the bottom step, he couldn't move his left arm at all, Dorr was gone, and so was the trunk he'd been trying to get down. The next time Roland saw him he was wearing the uniform of the United States Marine Corps.

The Marines sent Dorr to Japan, and when he was released and came home he stayed out west. Five years, six. Roland could still feel his left shoulder, and he could still hear Dorr shouting that he wasn't his father. That would explain a lot, but it wasn't true. For an instant that famous night, though, he and Dorr both believed it; and so now Roland had to wonder what what's-her-name—Diane—knew about that.

He was hot by the time he left the road and entered the lane that his house was on. Whom had he insulted at the post office by ignoring him when whoever it was remarked that it was warm? It wasn't important; they had written him off a long time ago. They didn't really expect to chat. It must have been Johnson. Johnson was right. It was more than warm. The hunters would have a bad time tomorrow morning. The woods were full of dry leaves that clattered with every movement and scared the deer off. Good luck to the deer, and to the hunters, too. He wouldn't want to be that Diane, a girl by herself hitchhiking alone tomorrow with the roads full of angry deer hunters, some of them drunk. She must be crazy. Still, there was the dog Edith said was with Diane. Maybe it protected her. Maybe it was a big dog. At the same moment he saw it, and it was.

★ ★ ★

The dog was lying in the dooryard dirt in front of Roland's house with its head on its front paws: a tall, black dog with a big head. On the ground beside it was a pile of clothing and a green pack with a back frame. The dog rose when Roland approached and sat up in its place by the clothes. It didn't offer to bark or growl, but it watched Roland as he came up the path to the house.

Roland didn't like dogs. The truth was, he was afraid of the big ones because he knew of many that were fierce. So he came slowly up to the dog, and when he was three feet from it he said, "Where is she?" The dog got up and sniffed at Roland's knee. Roland looked at the pile of clothes. There were blue jeans, a yellow T-shirt, a flannel shirt, and, he saw, underwear.

"She's swimming," he said. "Does she have a swimsuit?"

The dog looked at Roland, and when Roland started to walk on around the house toward the brook, the dog went on ahead of him.

"We'll see," said Roland.

Behind Roland's house the brook fell over ledges and filled a rock pool. In summer the water there was no more than a dark, sandy puddle, but in spring and fall the pool was five feet deep and you could swim in it if you could stand the cold. Dorr's girl was in the middle of the pool, evidently standing on the bottom. Her back was to Roland, and she seemed to be occupied in moving her arms through the water about her, gathering the water

with her arms, dreaming. Coming down the stream bank
from his house with the black dog in front of him,
Roland was looking down on her. He saw the girl was
naked. With the noise of the brook she didn't hear him
when he and the dog came down onto the pebbles
beside the water. Roland could see her hair lying on her
shoulders in dark, wet points and curls. He thought of
going back up to his house and waiting for her there.

Then the dog began barking at him. It backed
away from him, prancing on its front legs, barking and
snarling at Roland. "That's right," said Roland to the dog.
In the pool the girl turned and saw Roland. She waved
and smiled and called something he couldn't hear for
the brook and the dog. Roland wondered if he should
turn his back, but the girl began walking toward him
through the water, emerging from the pool before him,
every gleaming inch of her. Roland's eyes fled to the
pebbles, the trees, the dog, fled back to Dorr's girl.

What a size they were, women. Dressed, they
seemed small, but when they're naked you can see
they're not, they're our size. She was out of the pool
now, the last water ran off her arms and belly and down
her thighs to her feet. She was trying to calm the dog.

"That's enough now. He's okay. Really. Really."
She laughed, pushed her wet hair away from her ears.
She didn't try to cover herself; though it wasn't as if she
could have if she had tried; there was too much of her.
Roland was looking at the pebbles again, or resolutely
past the girl to the pool.

"Oh, boy," she said, "I'm embarrassing you, and
I'm sorry, but you're almost standing on my towel."

Roland bent and picked a white towel up from
the pebbles and handed it to the girl. She held it to her

front with her left hand so it hung down to her knees, but she didn't try to make it go around her. With her other hand she reached out to shake Roland's hand. "I'm Diane," she said. Roland held her hand, but he didn't think to shake it. "You cold?" he said.

"I am now," Diane said. "I wasn't in the water, the water was great. I was so hot. But it's cold now."

"Come on," Roland said, and turning quickly he went before her up the path to his house. There were two houses near the pool besides Roland's; two families and Roland lived there—nine people—and when Roland, Diane, and the dog filed up to the house, every one of them could see her bottom except him.

At the house Diane gathered up her clothes and went indoors. Roland and the dog stayed outside until she returned, dressed, but with her hair still wet and her feet bare. She stood on Roland's little side porch holding her wet towel. "Is there someplace where I can kind of hang this up?" she asked. Roland took the towel from her and hung it on a nail. "Oh, that's great," Diane said, shaking her head at him as though he'd just done something extraordinary, like throw an apple high in the air on a perfect curve so it fell right down the chimney.

Edith's letter had said the girl was a kid, hadn't it? She wasn't. Diane was probably thirty, Roland now saw. It was her ways that made her younger, and it was the dog with her. She was big, too, as tall as Roland, broad through the shoulders and hips, and she looked fit and strong. Her hair was straight, light brown when it was dry; her eyes blue or gray. She was kneeling with the dog, roughly stroking its coat down with her hand. Her hands were big, too, Roland saw, but her wrists were slender. Diane was telling him about the dog.

"His name is Denver," she said. "Because I got him in Denver, Colorado. Or just outside of Denver. I come from there. He's just a year old. He wouldn't have bitten you. He just barks. We kind of travel together."

"He was looking out for you," Roland said.

"What a great swimming hole," Diane said. "I was just so hot. I had to try it. I hope it was okay."

"It's no good when you need it."

"It isn't?"

"Goes dry in summer."

"Oh, boy. Well," Diane said, "but Dorr's told me about when you taught him to swim there. That's how I knew the river was there, before I came, because of Dorr telling me. You just kind of threw him in there one day, he said, so he'd learn to swim?"

Why had Dorr told her that? It hadn't been that way. What Diane was talking about might have finished like the night when Dorr left Roland on the stairs, except that Dorr had been only eight or nine.

When the children were little, Marjorie liked to take picnics to the brook. She insisted that Roland come, although he didn't see the sense of making a picnic within sight of your house. Anyway, he'd gone too, and the four of them were there: Marjorie, Roland, Edith, and Dorr. It was May or June: there was a lot of water in the pool. Roland had been sitting on a stone when Dorr came up behind him and jumped on his back. Roland tossed the boy over his shoulder into his lap and tickled him, Dorr shrieking but unresisting, his eyes shut tight. They wrestled that way. Then Roland stood, carrying Dorr, and walked over to the pool. "You're going in!" he said.

To the best of his knowledge he'd been fooling;

he hadn't intended to throw Dorr into the water. But as soon as he'd said, "You're going in!" Dorr's struggles in his arms changed. His shrieking stopped, and he fought Roland silently, with his eyes open, trying to hurt, afraid of the water, afraid of the man who held him. Roland didn't know how to break it off between them, and because he didn't know what else to do he went ahead and threw Dorr far out into the pool. "What are you *doing?*" Marjorie cried, and ran down the bank toward the water. But Dorr, who had gone under on hitting the water, rose to the surface and kicked over to the bank by himself. There his mother comforted him while Roland watched them from his place nearby and Edith began to cry. Now Dorr was telling his girl, Diane, that the episode had been a rough, country swimming lesson. Not by a long shot, it hadn't.

Roland supposed Diane wanted to eat. Daylight was about finished, and it had quickly become cool. They went in the house, but the dog stayed outside in the dooryard. Diane said she had her supper with her. Roland didn't know what she meant, but he made a fire in the stove, cut bacon, made tea. Diane said she would like tea. Heat from the iron stove filled the kitchen. Roland got out eggs and broke them into his frying pan with the bacon. But Diane said she'd have her own supper. When Roland brought his plate to the table she was there with a couple of pears and an apple and a box of crackers in front of her.

"Is that all you're going to have?" Roland asked her.

"Well, I'll have some tea," Diane said.

"Is that all? You can't live on that. Tea and pears. You mean you don't eat meat?"

"Well, yes. Well, no," Diane said. "Well, kind of. It's not that I don't like it. It's just that I don't think you should, or I don't think I should. Eat meat, all the time. It builds up poisons inside you. Also, I don't like to just barge in on you here and eat all your food."

"There's plenty," Roland said.

"Well, maybe you could kind of save some of yours, then," Diane said.

"Sure. Sure I can," Roland said.

"For Denver, after," Diane said. "That would be great. Thanks."

"For the dog?" Roland said.

When they had finished eating Diane took bacon and eggs out to the dog. Then she returned to the table, and she and Roland sat together. Roland was content. Diane talked about Dorr, though.

"I'm older than Dorr," Diane said. She laughed. "Do you want to hear all about him?"

Hell, no, thought Roland. No, I don't. "Where did you meet him?" he asked.

"In Denver," Diane said. "He was working in a bar there. You know, tending bar?"

A bartender. "What were you doing out there?" Roland asked her. He didn't want to hear about Dorr, but he did want to hear about Diane. He thought, from what he'd seen of Diane, that in her real life, when she wasn't passing naked through Vermont, she might have been anything from an exotic dancer to a female policeman or a schoolteacher.

"I was living with my sister," she said. "I was looking for a job, too. I'd been married, but that kind of went down the drain. So I was back in Denver looking for work. They have that big park there where the

government buildings are and everything, and that's
where I took Denver for his walk. Denver, the dog? And
one day Dorr kind of came up to me in the park. He
wasn't real nice. He thought I was my sister; he'd met
her the night before. I didn't like him, but it was funny,
because Denver did. And then I did—really liked him—
and I said, never mind getting a job. I'm going with him."

The dog was barking, not outside the kitchen
door, but farther off, down by the brook.

"Now, where is he?" Diane said. She rose from
the table and went to the door. Roland followed her.
Outside she said, "It's so dark."

"No, it isn't," said Roland. He stepped past Diane
and led the way down the bank to the brook where the
dog stood on the pebbles by the water and barked at
something across the stream.

Diane said to the dog, when they got down
there, "What's the matter? What is it?" The dog ran up
and down beside the water.

"He sees a deer," Roland said.

"Where?"

"In the orchard. You can't see them." Roland
stood close behind her so he spoke to her over her
shoulder.

"Orchard?"

"Across the brook," Roland said. He might have
whispered what he had to say into Diane's ear. "That was
my orchard, over there. It's grown up some."

Diane stood on the pebbles beside the brook
with her arms folded on her breasts and looked across
the water at the woods that Roland said was an orchard
populated now by deer. The dog was quiet.

"Dorr said you had an orchard."

"Well, we had," Roland said. "It's not ours now. I sold it. It's woods now. Nobody takes care of it, you see."

At nightfall this time of year deer came among the trees for the old apples and blowdowns. It had been twenty years since Roland had sold the orchard land. Dorr couldn't truthfully say he remembered when they had owned the orchard, but he told the girl his people were orchardists.

Roland had bought the place when he and Marjorie were first married: the orchard was to be their business. But it was never big enough to prosper, and if it had been, Roland had never been a good owner; he was meant to work for wages and keep his thoughts to himself.

He had expected spring frosts or autumn storms or bugs to ruin him in the orchard. They spared him. While the orchard was his, springs were early, autumns late. He killed the bugs. Yet he failed anyway, not from nature, but mathematically. It seemed he had too few apples. He'd never wanted a lot. He didn't want to be an apple king; his hopes had been modest, and still he had failed.

Roland sold the orchard when Edith was six or seven, Dorr a baby. He paid his debts. Then they had no money. Roland went to work in the woods, got hurt, quit the woods, and took a job at Jordan's sawmill in Ambrose. He took other jobs, winding up at Clifford's. He was doing what he could to keep the four of them, but he hadn't reckoned with Marjorie. She had been a schoolteacher before they married and she talked about going back to it. Roland didn't want her to. He believed she didn't really want to be a teacher again now that she was a wife. Indeed, she couldn't have been a teacher and a young mother both, not in Ambrose. That was as far as the subject went for Roland, but Marjorie had been thinking about their situation longer and harder than he. There was never enough money. There never would be while they both remained in Ambrose. Roland would never go anyplace else, and she would never ask him to. The rest was clear, then. Five years after they sold the orchard, Marjorie took both children and moved to Boston, to work.

She had a cousin there, and her cousin had written several times to say there was a teaching job for Marjorie at a school. "I believe we'll go," Marjorie said. It was that easy.

The children went with her. She couldn't leave them with Roland. He wouldn't have known what to do with them. Leaving Edith and Dorr, small children, with Roland would have been like giving him a velvet jacket or a microscope—any fancy, delicate thing that wasn't to be used hard. You'd find he had wiped his tools with the velvet, used the microscope to stop the door. Roland liked Edith and Dorr, Marjorie believed, but he didn't take care. Without her he would let them run naked in the woods until they starved or grew fur and turned into wild animals.

"Where does the river go?"

"Back of the village," Roland said. "It's a brook. We call it a brook."

Diane look upstream, where the brook fell between its dark banks into the pool.

"Up there," Roland said, "it comes from up the mountain." Roland told Diane how the brook began in a chain of little ponds up in the hills. Below the ponds was a falls. Years ago there had been a village up there with two mills, stores, good houses, a school. There had been twenty or thirty families living along the brook then, in a place in the woods that was now forgotten but that had once been as good a village as Ambrose. Now if you walked up there you could hardly tell there had ever been anything but forest. The cellar holes had grown in, and all that remained was the stonework of the mills' foundations alongside the brook, and the ruined mill-races.

"Did you go there?" Diane asked.

"I go there sometimes."

"I mean when the stores and people and every-thing were there."

"That was a hundred years ago." Roland pointed up the brook. "Below where the mills were, the brook goes by Alan Weatherhead's," he said. But Diane was looking across the brook again. Maybe she was looking for one of the deer to come out of the woods and show itself at the water side.

"He died the other day," Roland said.

"Oh, boy," Diane said. "Was he a friend of yours?"

"Friend of Dorr's," said Roland.

★ ★ ★

She was tired, she said—Dorr's girl, Diane. If she could spread a blanket on the sofa in Roland's kitchen she would be all right for the night. Her dog could stay in the kitchen with her or they could tie him outside.

"Outside is better," said Roland, who didn't like dogs much better now than he ever had. The three of them left the brook and went back up to the house. Roland found a blanket, and sheets, too.

"I don't really need them," Diane said. "I'll just kind of get under the blanket."

"Go ahead and take them," Roland said. "That's an old hair sofa. You don't want to lie on it."

"Thanks," Diane said. She made her bed on the sofa, and took Denver outside and tied him on the porch. When she came back into the kitchen Roland expected she'd start flinging off her clothes to prepare for bed, and he was about to leave her, but Diane got onto the sofa and under the sheet and blanket immediately, without undressing.

"Can I get all the way to Canada tomorrow?" she asked.

"I don't know. It's still a long way. Everybody thinks we're right near Canada up here, but we aren't. When are you going to start?"

"In the morning sometime."

"I can't give you a lift," Roland said. "No car."

"Oh, sure," Diane said. "You never had one. Dorr told me." She stretched her arms above her head and lay back on the sofa. "I can't wait to see him," she said. "I've just been following him around so long. My mother, all my friends, my sister, they think I'm crazy, I guess. I don't care," she laughed. "I hate to sleep alone," she said.

Roland turned out the light in the kitchen and went to the room where he slept, which was around the chimney on the same floor. He didn't need a light to undress and find his bed. Sometimes Roland didn't use the lights in his house at all from one day's end to another, but rose, went about, and slept by what daylight came into the house. He lay on his back in his bed and listened for some noise or movement from Diane in the kitchen. There was none.

She hates to sleep alone, she says, going to bed in his house. Now what kind of a thing is that for her to say? Could any man ignore that? Roland hadn't ignored it. Still, here he was, and here he'd stay. He worked hard. He slept easily. He hadn't much time in bed at night to wait for sleep, and what he had he preferred not to waste. He would use the time now to do what he'd wanted to do all day but had been prevented from by Diane's arrival: think about Alan Weatherhead.

It was your duty to think about the important dead if they were known to you. He had seen no grief at the cemetery that afternoon. At other buryings there he had seen grief that couldn't be contained. Did no one mourn Alan Weatherhead? What if Dorr had been at the cemetery? Would he have mourned, after everything that had happened? Would he indeed have mourned the harder for observing the others and finding his grief superior to theirs in the way of the young everywhere, who believe that only they have feelings?

No. Dorr had finished with Alan Weatherhead, the way he'd finished with Roland. He'd thrown Alan Weatherhead's good will in his teeth, and had done so in a way that was unmistakable. Dorr wouldn't be compelled by charity any more than he would be by force. He'd left Alan Weatherhead and Roland both behind, spit in both their faces. Give him that: Dorr was just as mean to everybody.

Still, that was later. Hadn't Alan Weatherhead liked Dorr? And certainly it wasn't the bad kid he'd befriended, but the boy who hadn't yet become the bad kid; a boy you could like, of whom Sybil Weatherhead, taking Roland aside in Clifford's one day, had said, "I wanted to tell you how much help Dorr is to my husband. Such a good-looking boy."

She had said it in her soft, hurried voice. She always talked as if she were short of breath. Such a good-looking boy. Even Marjorie wouldn't have said so much. They liked him. Why not? Alan Weatherhead had daughters, no sons. Also, he was an outsider; he could be fooled. Smart as he was, he didn't know everything. If he'd known more, he would have had Dorr jailed, which was what thieves expected. He didn't. He let Dorr off. He was a stranger, and so he didn't understand that letting Dorr off was no sign of anything, but a mistake.

Years before, it had been the same. When Roland was running the orchard, before either Edith or Dorr had been born, he found Alan Weatherhead one day sitting beside the brook tossing a fishing line out. Roland didn't mind telling him that you couldn't catch fish along there; Alan Weatherhead should go up to the dams.

"What dams?"

"The old dams," Roland told him. "The mills. Up at the old town."

"Where is it you mean?"

"Up the brook," Roland said.

"This brook?" Alan Weatherhead said. "I've been up this brook. There's nothing up there."

"There's a whole town up there," Roland said. "Those were the mills, and the only good fish in the whole brook are there, below the mills. You don't have to go up there. I don't care. I'm just telling you. I've lived here all my life."

"Steady," Alan Weatherhead said. "I know you have. And if you say it's there I'll have to go and look again, but I wonder if you're telling me a story here, with a whole town back in the middle of the woods. What's its name?"

"I don't know if it had a name," Roland said. "We call it the mills."

Roland didn't know whether Alan Weatherhead had ever figured out that he hadn't been fooling. He expected not; he expected Alan Weatherhead had forgotten about the whole exchange, for he wasn't really a fisherman, and he had no curiosity about the old ways of the town and countryside. He never knew what the village had been or why it was important. Alan Weatherhead sought rest in Ambrose. That was why, when Dorr had returned to live with Roland, Alan Weatherhead came to the house one day to ask if the boy wanted to earn a little money working around his place.

Marjorie had decided that Dorr should return to Ambrose to go to high school and live quietly with his father in their house. The reasons for that, and the arrangements for Dorr's return to Roland, were the subject of the only real talks he and Marjorie had had since she moved to Boston. The truth was, Marjorie couldn't handle Dorr. He fought her, he wouldn't obey, he ran away. Marjorie feared a boy as unruly as Dorr was in danger in the city. In Ambrose if he couldn't stay out of trouble he would at least be safe. Maybe living with his father would quiet him. Roland went along. He doubted if it was lawful to refuse to take in your own child.

Roland expected he would get some work out of Dorr, who was fifteen. But from the first Dorr let Roland see that he was not happy to be with him, that he was not enjoying himself and didn't expect to, that he would stay and follow his parents' plan for him exactly as long as it suited him to do so. At the same time Roland saw Dorr feared him, though he couldn't tell why, since Dorr was nearly his size already.

"I don't have to stay here after I'm sixteen," Dorr told Roland. "I don't have to go to school after I'm sixteen. It's the law."

I can send him away, that's what he's afraid of, Roland thought.

"What do you know about the law?" Roland asked.

Roland didn't get any work out of Dorr, but Alan Weatherhead did. At Weatherhead's, Dorr was more like an old-time hired man than like a kid you paid to do the chores. One day Roland saw Alan Weatherhead and Dorr in the side yard on either end of a crosscut saw working on Alan Weatherhead's winter firewood. Alan Weatherhead was puffing, while Dorr was going carefully so as to take the hardest strokes of the saw on himself. It made the long saw buckle and jerk. Alan Weatherhead and Dorr weren't much of a team for sawing. Alan Weatherhead wasn't strong; perhaps he had begun to fail by then.

That winter Dorr would shovel snow at Weatherhead's, and in the summer he dug their gardens. Often he'd eat dinner there and come home afterward. Once when Roland passed Weatherhead's he saw Dorr and Alan Weatherhead sitting together on kitchen chairs they'd brought out and set on the grass in front of the house. They were drinking beer and looking at the air, like a couple of bored old brothers with nothing to do.

For all Dorr would tell Roland about Alan

Weatherhead's house or what he did and heard there, Alan Weatherhead might have been his first sweetheart. Dorr was getting something at Weatherhead's, but Roland didn't know what. Once he asked Dorr whether he planned to join the Navy when he finished high school the next spring. Dorr said no, any service but that one, and Roland asked him why.

"Well, Alan Weatherhead," Dorr said. "He was in the Navy. He told me to stay away from it."

"He did?" Roland said.

"He said there's nothing the matter with the Navy except the ships," Dorr said. "The water. He said drowning is the worst death."

That was how Alan Weatherhead could impress Dorr, or any other kid who knew nothing. Still, he must have wanted to impress him. Sometimes a law-abiding man has need of a bad boy, but Alan Weatherhead had gone too far.

Toward the time Dorr had taken off, Roland was working at Clifford's. Alan Weatherhead had come to the store and started talking to him, asked him about Dorr's plans when he finished school.

"Well, it's up to him," Roland said.

"He's a nice boy," Alan Weatherhead said, as though Roland didn't believe it. Well, he didn't. "We think the world of him, the world. He doesn't have to go right into the Army because nothing else is possible."

"It's up to him," Roland said again.

Alan Weatherhead had wanted something from that talk, but he hadn't known how to go after it with Roland. It was Dorr who told Roland what Alan Weatherhead had been getting at.

"He thinks I ought to go to college," Dorr said. "He'll pay, he said."

"He will?" Roland said.

"Sure," Dorr said. "He's rich."

"What did you tell him?"

"I told him no," Dorr said. "I wouldn't waste my time." Dorr became excited. " 'Are you kidding?' I told him. I told him it's a bunch of crap—school. One's like another. 'Don't make me laugh,' I told him. 'If you've got all that money and don't know what to do with it, you can stick it up your ass. I don't want it.' "

"You didn't tell him that," Roland said.

"No," Dorr said. "I just said no. Then I left."

"What did he say?"

"Nothing," Dorr said. "He just stood there like a fish."

Dorr stayed away from Weatherhead's after that. Who knows where he went? All that spring Dorr had seemed as though he'd been burning up. Sometimes he came home at night drunk. Roland could handle him, though, by getting angry at him and shouting. Then the famous night came when that didn't work.

On his way out of town that night, Dorr went to Weatherhead's. Nobody was home, and the house was locked. Dorr broke a window in the kitchen, went in, grabbed some things. The things he took made no sense: a Waring blender, a copper colander, fireplace tools, a picture off the wall. He didn't care what he took. Then he left the house and drove off in one of Alan Weatherhead's cars. Alan Weatherhead called the constable the next morning. At about the same time, the stolen car turned up in the woods on the way to Brattleboro. It was out of gas. The car was banged up some. The articles that had been stolen from Weatherhead's were in the back.

It had to have been Dorr, but Alan Weatherhead

wouldn't make a complaint. He had his copper colander and the other things, he said. He had his car. He was willing to forget the matter. The constable went back and forth between Weatherhead's and Roland's house all day. The state police had been alerted. The constable was disgusted. "Law enforcement," he said. "It's nothing but a joke to some people." And he drove away fast in his car, which he'd paid his own money to have a blue light put on the top of.

But Dorr was gone, and Alan Weatherhead proclaimed himself content to fix his kitchen window, have his car repainted, and go on to other things.

"I never thought it was Dorr who did it," Alan Weatherhead told Roland later. If that was true, he was the only one who didn't. "What do you hear from Dorr?" Alan Weatherhead would ask Roland. "Where's Dorr now?"

Roland usually didn't know. Dorr had moved around. Now he was on his way to Canada to meet a woman who swam naked in your backyard and told you how much she hated to sleep alone. Roland yawned.

Out his window he could see one star. Soon it would be winter again. What was he waiting for? Wouldn't most men have gone in to Diane? He couldn't tell. Would Alan Weatherhead have gone to her? He thought yes, then no. Would Dorr, in his place now, go in and crawl onto that sofa with her? He must be a fast worker with women if he just picked this one up in a park. Still, maybe it wasn't that way. You had to find them somewhere. Maybe Dorr and Diane, having come together casually in that park, were wedded forever, as he was to Marjorie, whom there had been no need for him ever to meet since there had been no time in his life when he hadn't known her.

He thought about Diane bathing in the brook. When he'd come down the bank, she had known who he was, known him for Dorr's father. How? What had Dorr told Diane about him that had let her recognize him? Or what had Edith told her? Had they described him? How? What did he look like?

He and Dorr looked nothing alike. Did he look like Edith, then? What secret about him did his children know?

Roland slept. He dreamed. He was far up on the mountain, up the brook above the old mills, right at the ponds where the brook had its source. He was above the ponds, looking out over them. It was night. In the distance rose the hills and mountains around Ambrose. The sky was full of stars. When a star fell he could see its reflection flash in the dark, still surfaces of the ponds. The water in them was black, but he could see fish in their depths, the shadows of fish swimming there. Someone was near him, talking to him, saying, "Those are beaver-pond fish. They are nothing but mud trout. They're no good. If you eat them they taste muddy. You better leave them alone."

Now the dog was barking. It was barking outside the house. And there was a rapping on Roland's bedroom door. Diane was rapping on his door, calling in a soft voice, "Hello? Please wake up."

"What's the matter?" Roland called from the bed. Outside the dog still barked. From the orchard woods Roland heard a gunshot. The dog barked harder.

"Something is going on," Diane said through the door. "I'm sorry. I was kind of scared."

Roland looked out his window. It was still dark, but the single star was gone. It would be light in a while.

From across the brook came two more shots, three. Somebody was getting an early start. The dog was going crazy.

"Go on out and bring him inside," Roland said. "It's hunters. They're in the woods. Tomorrow is hunting season. Today."

"Are they shooting at the house?" Diane asked.

"They're shooting up the woods," Roland said. "They're probably half a mile off. Bring the dog in and go back to sleep."

"Okay. Oh, boy, I didn't know what was going on," Diane said on the other side of the door. "I was asleep. I thought a war had started."

"Deer hunters," Roland told her from his bed.

Diane went out on the porch and brought the dog, Denver, inside. He became quiet when he came indoors. The shooting from the woods had stopped. Diane got back into her bed on Roland's sofa.

Two hours later, when it was light, Roland came through the kitchen and let himself out the door to go to work at Clifford's. Diane still slept. The dog had climbed onto the sofa with her and lay beside her with its head on her stomach. It lifted its head and looked at Roland when he went quietly by. As he shut the door behind him it occurred to Roland that Diane, who hated to sleep alone, hadn't had to. By the time he got back at the end of the afternoon she would be gone.

★ ★ ★

There were hunters in the woods. Their trucks were parked beside the brook, beside the road Roland took to the village. He heard their guns. At Clifford's nobody knew that Diane had passed through; evidently Roland's neighbors by the rock pool had missed the show yesterday evening, after all.

Around lunchtime the two Robinson boys came into Clifford's. They had been hunting in the woods back of Roland's house since before dawn. They hadn't seen a deer. They were talking with young Clifford. The Robinsons expected they'd go up the brook after lunch and try it there. They'd go up by the old mills.

"Don't waste your time," young Clifford said. "There's nothing up there."

Roland was on his knees on the floor putting canned tomatoes into a low shelf. He came up off the floor and went around to the counter, holding a can of tomatoes as though he was about to throw it at young Clifford's head. Young Clifford and the Robinsons looked at him.

"You're a young fool," Roland shouted. "You don't know a goddamned thing. There were a hundred people living up there!"

6

Before
HE Went
Out WEST

There was nothing to do in Ambrose. I joined the rescue. A rich man had about died because the ambulance from Brattleboro took an hour for the trip, so he bought Brattleboro's older ambulance and set it up in Ambrose as Dead River Rescue. How is that for the name of something that is meant to save your life?

Volunteers did all the work, raised money to buy equipment. Someone gave the use of a garage. The ambulance itself was a problem. Ambrose and the next towns along the Dead River put in each year for its upkeep, but that ambulance was old when it was new, and it couldn't last forever. Then one night Paul Law and I burned up her brakes coming around Ambrose Corner with Rowena Pinto having her baby in the back. After that the ambulance was, you might say, mechanically never the same again. And then, suddenly, the whole program sighed and died. The towns were good for gas and tires, but they weren't about to go all the way in for

a new ambulance. Anyway, the roads from Brattleboro
had been improved since the rescue had started; there
wasn't a need any longer even for distant little towns to
have their own ambulances. Dead River Rescue broke
up, and then there was *really* nothing to do in Ambrose.

I had a friend who had gone out West, so I
decided I'd try it out there, too. Wyoming. Wyoming is
not this story. This is a rescue story about something
that happened, that I saw, when I was on the ambulance.
Every word is true.

★ ★ ★

Dead River Rescue ran on will and nerve, and not on
science. We had a good first-aid box on the ambulance,
and we had one of those stretchers for people with back
injuries. We had some other stuff. We had two or three
members who had been trained by the Red Cross and
who tried to teach the rest of us. But mainly we had a
big taxicab with a bed in the back. Our aim was to get
our man on the stretcher in the back of the ambulance
and get him strapped down so he couldn't roll off, and
then drive like hell for the nearest hospital. Don't laugh;
mostly it worked. We saved some people. Before Dead
River Rescue, if you lived back in the hills around
Ambrose or one of those other little towns and you got
sick or badly hurt, you were probably dead. With us at
least you had a terrifying chance.

We trained two nights a week. We drank coffee.
We washed the ambulance. We arranged the garage
where it was kept. We drove in parades. We answered
one or two calls a month. I guess a third of them were
from houses where someone had peacefully died. To the

younger men on the ambulance those calls were cake. They were cake to me—not fun, no, but easy. You can't make a mistake, because whoever it is is already gone, and there's nothing you don't want to look at, as there is in a bad car crash. You're just transportation. Everybody wins, I mean, unless you know the dead person; and even in a town the size of Ambrose, you never do.

We thought it was going to be a trip of that kind when Harvey Lombard and I took the ambulance out one Friday morning in June, answering a call from a woman at a house halfway up Round Mountain in North Ambrose.

Harvey had been on the rescue since it started. He knew what to do. He had talked to the woman. She sounded all right. Her husband had quit breathing. She gave directions to their place. Ussery was their name.

"Know them?" Harvey asked me when we had gotten underway.

"No," I said. I was driving. "Do you?"

"Seen him," Harvey said. "They're new. Bought Coalheaver's place up there—I don't know, last year, the year before. Cash transaction."

"Where from?" I asked Harvey.

"I heard," he said. "Don't remember."

Harvey was fifty or fifty-five, a little shorter than I am. He had big arms and shoulders and an enormous behind. That comes from too much riding on small seats. Harvey was a substitute rural letter carrier, and he drove a bulldozer that he and his son owned and hired out. So he was bouncing around in some vehicle all day long, and it made his bottom spread, I guess. He was also a carpenter, a deer hunter, an Army veteran, a fattener of spring pigs—a man who, for example, probably hasn't been to a movie in thirty years. "Why should I go to the movies?" asks Harvey. "Full of kids making noise. You can't hear." How do you know, Harvey, if you never go? "Anyway, they all come on the TV," says Harvey. In a few years he'll start going to the movies again, with his grandchildren, and then he'll go every Saturday until he gets too old to move.

We took twenty minutes to reach the house. From the highway you got on a dirt road that branched once or twice, then went back up Round Mountain. The road went uphill through dark woods, came out on a level with open fields and a house and barn, went up through woods again, then came out. In some of the openings the fields were full of brush and little trees, in others they were mowed or grazed by cows that we passed. Once in the woods we went over a bridge that the brook had tried to wash away that spring. Four men from the town were fixing it, getting ready to pour a new abutment. It was just a little bridge. The men waved us on over, and when we'd passed I looked back. They had stopped work and stood in the road looking after us, wondering where up there we were going, where the trouble was.

We found the house. It was up on the bank, set close to the road as the old houses all are. Its front was in the sun, and all around the house orange lilies grew in crowded beds. An old wooden garden chair, painted white, was on the grass out front, between the house and the lilies. There was no car at the house, no dog. The house was old, but it had paint and a new roof. Harvey knew the place. He went to a shed at the back where there was a door into the house. Harvey knocked on the door. Nobody came. He tried to open it. The door was locked. Harvey thumped on the door with his fist and rattled the latch. The house was still. Then I knew this was going to be a bad one after all, and not cake.

"Another door around the side," I said.

"Go look," Harvey said. I went around the house. I ran. The side door was locked. I went around to the front door, which faced the road. That door was locked. I went back to the shed. I'd been clear around the house. I told Harvey the place was locked tight.

"Give me some room," Harvey said. He stepped back from the door and, raising his right knee, he kicked the door hard just above the latch with his weight behind the flat of his foot. The door flew open and banged against the wall inside, and the broken latch was thrown across the room and fell on the floor. We went into the kitchen.

"Hello?" Harvey called. "Who wants the ambulance?" Nobody answered.

We went through the kitchen to a closed room set up as a parlor where through the windows you could see the lilies that grew around the house and beyond them the road and a bright meadow on the other side; then we went on toward the front of the house through a door to a stairs. At the bottom Harvey stopped, and I think he was going to call out again, but then he changed his mind. We went up. Harvey made a lot of noise going up the stairs ahead of me.

Upstairs to our right the house was unfinished: dark rafters overhead and walls with the studs and the rough outside wall showing, weak light from two windows at the end of the house. To the left was a room that had been finished: plastered, wallpapered. It was a bedroom. On the bed, a narrow bed, was a man, dressed, laid out on his back, and on a chair beside the bed, facing him, a woman sat. Harvey and I went in. There was a smell in the room like flowers or soap.

Harvey went quickly to the bed on the side opposite the woman. He never looked at her. Harvey picked up the man's hand and patted it. Holding it, he laid his other hand on the man's forehead. Then he let the hand go. It flopped back down on the bed in that bad way.

The woman in the chair hadn't been watching Harvey. Even when we had come into the room, she hadn't turned her head. So calm. She knew he was gone, she had known when she called the ambulance. She sat looking out the window that was beside the head of the bed. "You were quick coming," she said.

Harvey went around the bed near her chair and bent over the man on the bed. He tilted the man's head back and opened his mouth. Harvey then took a breath, put his mouth to the man's mouth, and tried to blow air into him. He took another breath and tried again. It was like blowing down a long, empty pipe. Harvey will work on you that way for half an hour if he thinks he can bring you back, but he doesn't waste his time. He quit. He stood up.

The woman hadn't looked while Harvey bent, puffing, and pressed his mouth so eagerly on her husband's. At that sight, I swear she turned a little pink. I've noticed how embarrassment, more than any other feeling, will sneak in and take over at times when it's quite crazy it should because so many more important things are happening, like now for her. Though any other time, well, it's true Harvey isn't like a fellow you'd expect to find kissing a fellow.

Now I saw that the woman's mouth and chin were trembling, her face was falling down like a little kid's who is about to cry. Oh, boy, I thought. She tried not to give way. And she didn't—she didn't cry. Still looking out the window before her, not at the dead man on the bed, and not at us, she opened her mouth and screamed. I looked the other way. She drew breath and screamed again. She raised her fists together and beat them gently down into her lap, and when she did that she cranked the screaming up another notch. Loud, painful screams came out of her mouth. She wasn't crying. Her eyes were dry, open, looking out the window, and her screams now sounded ragged, as though if she kept on screaming so hard something in her throat would tear out and fly through the window.

I don't know where we were supposed to go from there: Harvey and I standing on either side of the bed, the man lying on it, and the woman in her chair on Harvey's side screaming and staring and beating her hands into her lap; but then I saw another man had come into the room. He was an old man with white or gray hair, but big, taller than I am, broader than Harvey. He was dressed in heavy, dark clothes. He ignored the woman, as Harvey had. With her screaming, he went to the bed on my side. I got right out of his way. He looked at the dead man, then bent and put his hand on the dead man's head as Harvey had, but roughly, as though he'd roughly muss his hair. Impatiently he shoved the dead man's head to one side and stood up. He looked at Harvey. Harvey nodded to him. Harvey knew him.

The woman's screaming filled the room and beat on the walls and on the air in the room. She would not stop. I needed to get out of there right away. The big old man was standing beside me. He took hold of my arm, looked at Harvey.

"He's getting ready to fold up," he said.

"I'm all right," I told them.

"Go down and get the stretcher, Ben," Harvey said. "Get the stretcher," he said louder, over the woman's screams. I left the room and went to the stairs. I hope I didn't run.

Outside I opened the rear doors of the ambulance and pulled the stretcher out. But then I didn't go back in the house. I took the stretcher and went and sat down in the sunlight on the garden chair out front. Bees were in the lilies there, and the boards of the seat were warm from the sun's being on them. I heard the woman still screaming inside. Where I was her screams weren't loud. But she bore down so hard for those screams. Your girlfriend used to scream that way at a scary movie. But your girlfriend screamed partly out of what was happening in the movie, partly out of being there in the dark with you, and partly out of too much excitement and life to hold in.

She had stopped. I knew I ought not to stay away any longer. I picked up the stretcher and carried it into the house. Upstairs it looked like Harvey was about finished. He was getting the papers ready, writing on the top of a dresser in one corner of the room. His back was to the bed. The older man was kneeling on the floor in front of the woman. He had fetched her a cup of water. It was on the bed beside her. She still sat in her chair. The man patted her hands, which she held together in her lap. He had her calmed down some. He was talking to her.

"They can take him now. They'll take him down to Landrum's, and you can go on down there later. I'll call Olivia. Do you want me to call Olivia?"

The woman nodded her head, but I don't think she knew what he was saying. I was afraid she would start screaming again. The man was looking at her face. She raised one of her hands from her lap, and he picked up the cup of water from the bed and put it in her hand. The woman drank, and then she brought the cup carefully out, away from her lips, and he took it from her hand and put it back on the bed. She was blind. Oh, boy, I thought. I guess Harvey had seen it when I was out of the house, or maybe he had known. What is she going to do now?

"You or she can sign this, and then we can go," Harvey said to the man, and he handed him the papers he'd been working on. The woman shook her head. She kept on shaking it, slowly, in a way I didn't like to see. Nobody wanted her to get started again. The older man got to his feet beside her chair and took the papers from Harvey.

"Take him now," he said. "I'll bring her down this afternoon, or Olivia will, and we'll sign everything then. Leave the papers here for now. Can't you do that?"

"I guess so. I don't recall your name," Harvey said to the man. "We'll need your name now, anyway." Harvey was embarrassed at not remembering the man's name.

"Harrison Bean," the man said.

Now Harvey was in a hurry. "All right," he said, and I put the stretcher on the bed beside the dead man. Together Harvey and I got him onto it and carried him out of the room and down the stairs. The older man came after us. In the kitchen he stopped us. The blind woman stayed upstairs.

"Who busted the door?" the man asked.

Harvey and I each had an end of the stretcher with the dead man on it. We stood there with him slung between us. He was a weight. We just looked at the older man, I guess.

"Doors were all latched," Harvey said after a moment. "We knocked, but she wouldn't come down. We had to break in."

"How is she going to come down?" the man asked. "She can't see her way. He took care of all that."

"Well," Harvey said, "we still had to get in."

"You tore the latch right off and busted the frame as well," the man said. "It's split right up and down."

"We had to."

"Well, God damn it to hell," the man said.

I don't think Harvey believed this conversation was possible. He didn't answer. He led, and we went out by the broken door, through the dark shed, and out to the ambulance.

"Somebody is going to pay for that door," the man called after us.

We put the dead man in the back of the ambulance and shut the doors. Harvey and I both got in front, and I started the engine and rolled onto the road. The old man didn't show himself. Down the road in the woods where the bridge had washed, the four men were sitting beside the road in the shadows, taking a break. They were sitting in a row. They watched us go by. One of them waved.

"His name isn't Bean," Harvey said. "I know him, but I can't say his name. Obie will be able to. Used to work for Whitman out at Pied Brook. Van Amstel, the constable years ago, is some relation of his. Can't say his name right now, but it isn't Bean. Nobody around here by that name."

"Well, why would he give you a wrong name?" I asked.

"Don't know," said Harvey. "Some of those old guys back in there don't have both oars in the water. Wish I could think of his name."

We were off the mountain and back on the paved road in open country, and I can show you where we were passing that sign—GIFTS JUST AHEAD, RIDDLE'S 10,000 VERMONT GIFTS—when we hit a hole and took a big bump, and the dead man in the back sat up and said, "What the hell is going on here?"

I stepped on the brakes too hard, and Harvey and I about went through the windshield, but the man on the stretcher was still up, and now he was trying to get out of the strap around his waist that held him down. The ambulance skidded when I put on the brakes, and we almost lost the road. "Jesus, will you look out? You'll kill us all," Harvey said. When we were under control again he went in back with the man. "You are all right," Harvey said. "You were sick, but you're okay. Take it easy." He was looking the man over, but he wasn't touching him.

"I've heard of this," Harvey said. "How do you feel?" he asked the man on the stretcher.

"Where's Edith?" the man asked.

We took him to Brattleboro to the hospital. We left him there. If they flew in a lot of high-priced doctors and religious men to go over him, I never heard about it.

I guess it was that fall Paul Law and I wrecked over the ambulance's brakes on Ambrose Corner. It's sitting there today in Law's yard. Paul has it up on blocks, and he's taken the wheels off. He'll get it running and then sell it to some kid. The rescue broke up. There was nothing to do in Ambrose. I moved to Wyoming. There are so many things I don't know. The man who said his name was Bean, the blind woman up Round Mountain, the man who died, Harvey—I didn't want to see any of them for a while. They all know more than me.

7

DREAMING of AFRICA

A kid came with Leet to fix my wall and shunned my own boy—who wanted to be his friend—though Leet's kid, Wayne, wasn't more than a couple of years older than my boy, and is in fact a cousin of his, somehow, for Leet is some kind of cousin of mine.

He used to chase me around our schoolyard, and when he caught me he'd throw me down, though I was a little older and always taller than he. Later, when we were no longer in school together, you'd have to say Leet and I went into different orbits. Now, it happens, we converge once more, and Amy, knowing Leet for the first time, says that she sees some of him in me, some of me in him. She wouldn't have, then.

Leet was a hell-raiser when he was younger. He wasn't bad tempered, but he fought. He was a recreational fist-fighter, so to speak, at county fairs, behind taverns, and alongside roads by night. Then he'd drive the back roads drunk, and crash. He has a scar on his forehead and scalp from going through the windshield of one of his cars that went off a curve and landed in a brook down below some dark road. Leet's nickname for a time was Buick, for all the cars he crashed.

Sometime he got married and started having kids, whom it looked like he'd never get to know well. But then he calmed down, quite abruptly, as though somebody had taken him off the stove. It wasn't marriage that gentled Leet; it wasn't fatherhood. I don't know what it was.

He became a patriot—not an American patriot, but a patriot of Ambrose, Vermont, his town. Life anyplace else was mean and dangerous, Leet insisted. He had seen something of the country: before he married, Leet had been in the Navy. He had gone out to wherever they send you; I've forgotten where—somewhere away. He was discharged, came home, stayed. I wonder if at some time it didn't occur to Seaman Leet, in New London or Great Lakes or Pensacola, that he could leave Ambrose and take up life in any of a million foreign places; and I wonder if that didn't make him uneasy.

In any case, Leet became Ambrose's tireless defender. Does someone say something about the condition of the town roads? "There are two hundred miles of roads just in this town," Leet says. "You didn't think it was that many? It's a little better than two hundred. The road crew is five men and two temporaries. I've worked on the road crew. They don't get paid much. They do a job. The roads here are good."

For a minute it looks like Leet is working up to a fight again, as in days gone by, but then he settles down.

"I don't need to live anyplace else," Leet says. "Nobody does, if they knew. They've got everything here. Of course," Leet says, "it's changed a lot. A lot of new people are coming in."

Proclaiming his love for his home, and for his life there took the place of hell-raising with Leet, and if it made him a bit of a bore, well, perhaps it saved his life, too, given the way he was going before he discovered patriotism.

Leet does some of everything. He's a builder, mason, helper on any job, car mechanic, logger, cord-wood cutter, deer hunter. Getting into his forties, though, Leet's beginning to look a little beat up. He was never a handsome boy, or man, but he always had a quick, incurious eye. He has that gray eye still, but he used to be full of motion too, and now he looks as though his movements begin to be painful. Leet finds his joints are stiff in the mornings. The men can start to stiffen up young when they work all day out-side, as Leet does. Once they get old and lame to a certain point, though, they get no worse; and they may last forever.

The wall Leet came to fix was a retaining wall, waist-high, of round stones. It held the bank the house sat on. On the bank above it were day lilies. When the snow went out, the middle stretch of wall fell and the stones were tumbled about before the wall. We turned over some of the stones. The smallest were the size of a coconut, the biggest, a footstool. I couldn't stir the largest ones. I got both hands under one of them, braced my feet near my hands, and bent my weight against the stone. The stone didn't move, its weight was fearful.

I wanted to make it move. I sent Neddy for a timber we could use as a lever. He got a two-by-four and shoved it under the stone, put a smaller stone behind the stick. Then together we leaned to it, and I seemed to sense a shift somewhere, but I feared the hammer's stroke beginning in my chest, and I released the stone, turned, and sat on it. Neddy was looking at me. I shook my head.

My wife called from the house, "John? Call Leet, John," for I had said days ago, when we saw the state the wall was in, "Leet does that work."

"Do you think it moved?" I asked Neddy.

"I don't know. No," he said.

"Well, it doesn't matter," I said. "Would you take the two-by-four back?" Neddy took it away.

"John?" Amy called again.

"I'm coming," I said. From my seat on the stone I looked into the bank where the stones had fallen away. In the darkness behind the wall the pale roots of the lilies hung. I stood, went into the house. I called Leet. He wasn't home. I talked to his wife.

He came days after I called, rolling up the driveway too fast, he and his kid bouncing around on the seat of his truck. Amy was away, which would be a disappointment to Leet, who admired her.

Leet's son, Wayne, had a conscript look about him, as though he might not be happy to be along with his father that day. Leet got down from the truck and came over to me, but the kid took his time. He was slow to get out of the truck, and when he did he left the door open. He followed Leet, but at a distance. Leet turned to him.

"Get the door," he said.

Wayne went back around the truck. He shut the door, softly. Then he came around and sat on the front of the truck, looking up the hill, not at us.

"Come on," Leet said.

Wayne got up from his seat and started toward us, but Leet didn't wait for him. The three of us went over to the wall, Wayne staying behind a little.

We stood around the tumbled stones at the foot of the wall.

"She said you've got some wall trouble," said Leet.

"It came right down," I said. "The ice broke it up."

"The son of a bitch isn't founded right," Leet said. "It's just sitting on the soil. Maybe it is dug in some. Nothing can stop ice unless it's on ledge." He kicked one of the stones. "It will all have to come down. I don't know if we'll be able to finish it for you today."

Leet's boy stood with us, looking at the ground before his feet, at the fallen stones. I had a look at him. A darker Leet. He didn't say anything.

"You don't have to hurry," I said. I said to Leet's boy: "I know you're both busy."

Wayne's eyes stayed down mostly. He didn't answer or look at me, but when he heard me say something to him he raised his eyes from the ground and looked up past the house to the meadow and the woods behind.

I looked up at the house. Neddy's face was in the window of his room, above us. I waved to him. "Come on down," I called. Neddy's face went away, and I thought he was coming down.

"Are you all by yourself today?" Leet asked.

"Amy's in Boston. She'll be back tonight," I said, for I believed Leet and the others expected my wife to move out on me for good sooner or later, and had expected it since we had come back to Ambrose.

"Why would anybody want to go to Boston?" said Leet.

Yes, he was put out at missing Amy. He would have liked to have seen her today.

"Leet fancies you," I'd told Amy.

"I know," she said. "I wouldn't think I'd be his type."

"Lust knows no types."

"Doesn't it?" said Amy. "Goodness."

Leet wasn't a man for women. I doubt he'd known many; I'd say he's the farthest thing from a seducer. Still, he has eyes, and I know he likes to look. He likes Amy. He likes her hair. Leet and the other men around Ambrose have the old-fashioned idea that red-haired women are special—less moral than others, I guess, and more fun. And Amy played the part, sure she did. She was easy with Leet, which he also liked in her. His own women were too silent for him. 'Hello, Leet, how are you? Keeping out of trouble, Leet?' she would say. 'Nope,' Leet said, looking up at Amy from whatever he was doing. 'Not me. What about you?'

Neddy came around the house on our left. He jumped from the wall down to where we were. It was a bigger drop than he had expected. Neddy landed hard, and his pale hair fell down over his forehead. He pushed it back on his head, and I saw from the way he did this that his jump off the wall was something he'd wanted the older boy to see. Wayne hadn't seen it, though, or if he had he gave no sign. He was still studying his feet. He looked as though he wished he were with them, down in the grass, out of our attention, or up in the woods back of the house, where he had let his eyes rest a moment before.

Neddy's knees were bare. He made Wayne look like a man—like Leet, in fact. Wayne was a troublesome kind, and like other troublesome kids his age, he was big. His hands were as big as mine; his wrists, heavier. Neddy looked like a sandpiper beside him. Wayne was going to be bigger than his father.

"Best get to it," Leet said. He went up to the wall, then turned to Neddy. "You watch your feet, now," he said. Neddy hadn't expected Leet to speak to him. He didn't move.

"Me?" he said.

"*You,*" said Leet, with a laugh. "Mash your foot for you." He laid his hand on a stone at the top of the wall and pulled it out. The stone he had moved and two beside it sprang out of the wall and fell down to the ground. You could feel the ground shudder with their weight hitting it.

I went back to the house. Neddy followed me.

"Why don't you stay out?" I asked him. "Maybe you could give them some help."

"I don't think they need help," Neddy said.

"There is always something that's a help on a job like that. Go ahead. Ask Leet."

"Could you ask him?" Neddy said.

"No," I said. "You go ahead."

Neddy returned to the wall, and I went inside. From the house I could see Leet and Wayne working before the wall. I could hear the bumping and cracking of the big stones as they pulled them down out of the wall. Neddy was beside them, by Leet, who was talking to him but looking at what he was doing, not at Neddy. Wayne was to the side; he wasn't saying anything. In a moment Neddy went off, behind Leet and Wayne, and started hauling at one of the fallen stones that lay at some distance from the others.

Neddy was ten that spring. I wondered what he made of life so far. He was born in the European clinic in Dar es Salaam. It was a crazy place, a frontier town, really, beside the Indian Ocean, a metropolis of exhausted imperialism. I didn't like it and Amy didn't like it, but I'm not sure about Neddy. He will have African dreams from time to time today, and they are good dreams, of the trees that grew in front of our garden wall, of white stone buildings. In Dar es Salaam German civilizers had reared churches white as sugar beside the splendid harbor.

When I got sick and we had to leave Africa, we weren't sorry, we said, except for the sake of Neddy's friends. He had exotic companions. They were all colors, spoke all tongues. I remember Robert, and Iffy, who was Lebanese, I think; Hanne; and Jean-Jacques, whom Amy must call JJ. With Neddy, they raced in and out of the shadows in our small, low house. We had to keep the shutters closed all day against the heat.

I couldn't understand a word any of those children said, and I don't know how well they understood one another. Nevertheless, their games together seemed to rest on complex premises and formulas that they had perfected among themselves, and that none of them hesitated over. I remember Neddy, on the run through the front room, shouting, *"La bombe atomique!",* JJ right after him. Neddy's pals in Dar, he had pals there.

Africa will always be to me a child's world. Ambrose is different. In Ambrose there are few kids, and they are in the village, and Neddy doesn't know them.

Amy and Neddy talk together at his bedtime.

"Are you lonely, baby?"

"No, Pea," he says.

"Have you got enough to do?"

I don't know what he does all day, with nobody around. Does he think?

"What are you thinking about?" Amy asks Neddy.

He's quiet. He's a quiet kid. I don't know how much help he's going to be to me, in the way I saw Wayne was helping Leet. They were down behind the wall, out of sight, taking out the lower courses of stones. Wayne would stand and carry a stone out of the way, or if it was a little one, he'd turn and throw it. He threw them to land behind where he and Leet were working. Neddy was back there.

Several of the stones Wayne threw back landed close to him. When one of Wayne's stones hit near him, Neddy started up expectantly. He would have gone on in whatever game with the stones Wayne wanted the two of them to be in, but Wayne ignored him. He never hailed Neddy or said anything at all. He was already back at the wall with his father.

Wayne could help his father there, and with any other job, because of his size and strength, and because of an inherited will to competence that Neddy didn't get. Neddy doesn't have that, but he doesn't need it. He has what he needs—a willing heart, and a measure of indulgence from his betters. If Wayne doesn't want to help on jobs any more, Leet will yell at him until he goes along. If he has to, he'll beat him. I'll never lay a hand on Neddy, I know.

★ ★ ★

"How have you been feeling?" Leet asked me. "Pretty well?" I had brought two bottles of beer down to the wall. Leet and I drank them. Wayne and Neddy weren't around, and I was about to ask Leet what had become of them when he asked me how I had been.

"I don't know," I said. "The other day I tried to put some of that wall back up myself. I couldn't move the stones, the big ones. I don't have the strength any-more I guess is it."

I had never had Leet's strength, but he said, "Oh, God, I know it," as though I'd been talking about us both, our common decline, instead of just my own.

Leet set his beer bottle down in the grass, and started looking at the wall again and the stones scattered over the ground before it. He knelt and laid his hand on one.

"I'd think you'd wear gloves for that work," I said.

"You can't," said Leet. He laid his hand on an-other stone. "You have to be able to feel them."

"What happened to your help?" I asked.

"You're talking about those kids?" Leet said. "Well, you wouldn't say they were much help, exactly, no. Your boy would help if he could, but he's too small. That other one—" Leet stood up and stepped long, over the stones on the ground to the other side of the area where they lay fallen—"he's gone off somewhere."

Leet moved among the fallen stones. He touched them, he shifted them, he looked from them to the wall, but as yet he made no move to replace any stone there.

"He's a big boy," I said.

Leet wasn't going to have a conversation with me on the subject of his son. Wayne was twelve. He was the only boy. There were three girls, his sisters, one older and two younger than Wayne. I didn't know them. There were those unknown, good girls, and there was Wayne, the son. He was not an easy boy. He wasn't in school today, because he'd socked his teacher. It was not the wild swinging of a powerless kid, either: he'd knocked her down and broken her nose. The school had kicked Wayne out for the remainder of the year. They had never been able to handle him. Now Wayne was going around with Leet, since Leet's wife couldn't stand to have him in the house with her. Wayne's misbehaving looked like it was getting beyond high spirits. He stole. He ran wild at night and looked in people's windows. Once he set a cat on fire. "Why doesn't somebody get some help for him?" Amy had asked.

"Boys are mean," I told her.

"Neddy isn't," she said. "You weren't."

"You don't know I wasn't."

She was right though. I hadn't been. Neddy isn't. Even Leet, I think, was never as bad as Wayne. In a bigger town Wayne would have come to the attention of the police before now.

Leet stooped over a large stone. He got his hand under the edge of it, then straightened up and rolled the stone into the bottom of the wall.

"He is some big," Leet said. "He doesn't get away with anything at home, I can tell you that."

Leet was looking at the wall, wiping his hands down the sides of his trousers. "But, hell," he said. "That school. They don't do anything. They send him home. I told them if he hit the teacher, she could damned well hit him back."

"I heard she was on the floor," I said.

"She wasn't on the floor," said Leet, but he didn't really know.

"What are you going to do?" I asked him.

"Nothing," said Leet. "A couple more years and he'll be through with school. Then he goes into the Navy, or the Army. I don't care. He'll come back and see just what he's got here—his home, his family—and he'll see how he's wasting it when he ought to thank God for being born here and not somewhere else, and having this place for home." He rolled another stone up to the wall.

"It happened to me the same way," said Leet.

★ ★ ★

I went to find Neddy and Wayne. Around the side of the house I saw Neddy sitting under a tree. The tree was an oak with low branches. Wayne wasn't with him. Well, why should he be? Wayne wasn't a kid you'd want your own to be thrown in with; but nevertheless I caught myself in the assumption that he and Neddy were marked for partners.

Why? Why should I have thought those two were to be allies? No creatures are more different than different kinds of kids.

I went inside and walked among our rooms. There was no newspaper yet, and nothing else I wanted to read. I went to get another bottle of beer for myself, drink not being one of the things I feared. From the kitchen I could see the tree and Neddy beneath it. I watched him from the window. There was nothing I had to do. The doctor in Dar es Salaam, when I went to him about the hammer in my heart, had told me I must leave Africa. Later another doctor in Boston had said, "Take it easy. Watch the grass grow. Enjoy life." When have I not enjoyed life?

Neddy was coming down the stairs behind me. He had left the tree and come indoors before my eyes, and I hadn't seen him do it. Now he was hurrying downstairs, his step light, quick. I went to meet him. He was just at the door, on his way out again.

"What are you doing?" I asked him.

"Get my helmet." Neddy was a little out of breath.

"What do you want that for?"

"He's up the tree."

I didn't understand him. "Be careful if you're climbing up there," I said.

"I'm not climbing," said Neddy. "He won't let me."

"Who won't?"

"Wayne."

"Where's he?" I asked Neddy.

"In the tree," he said. "He won't let me go up."

"It's your tree. Do you want me to go out and tell him he has to let you up?"

"No." Neddy shook his head. "He won't say any-thing. Why can't he talk? Won't they let him?"

"I don't know," I said.

"I have to get back," Neddy said. He went out the door and ran toward the tree. We had an old British Tommy helmet from somewhere that had become Neddy's. He had it now, carried in his hand as he ran.

I went to the window where I'd watched Neddy before. I wanted to see Wayne. He was in the tree, twenty feet up. I'd missed him earlier. Wayne was stand-ing with his legs spread wide apart and braced against two branches, his body leaning back against the tree trunk. The afternoon sun was beginning to get down behind the upper branches of the tree; on his perch Wayne was a dark mass gently swaying. He was doing something, but I couldn't quite tell what—fishing in his pants, it could have been. Neddy stood by the tree's root, looking up into the branches at Wayne. He was wearing the helmet.

I couldn't hear that either Neddy or Wayne was speaking. Wayne hadn't said a word all day. It occurred to me that he might have been forbidden to speak to anyone as punishment for his misbehavior in school. That didn't sound to me like a measure Leet would take, but possibly Leet's wife was behind it.

In the tree, Wayne made a sudden motion with his arm, then another. I saw him. Again Wayne's arm went up, then quickly down. I saw that he was hurling something down at Neddy. Wayne threw, and the branches he stood on shook with the violence of his throw. Damn him, whatever he had he was throwing it down as hard as he could at Neddy, who still waited below him.

I tried to open the window I stood at, but it stuck part of the way up. I stooped to get my face at the opening so I could yell at them. The air of spring came in onto my face, and with it the sound of Neddy's laughter. I didn't call out. I looked again. Neddy was at the foot of the tree, his head bent.

"*Missed,*" he called out. "*Missed then, too.*"

Then came a loud, ringing sound. One of Wayne's rocks, or whatever it was he threw, had hit the steel helmet Neddy wore.

"*Hit,*" Neddy called. Above him, Wayne dug in his pocket for another round and looked between his feet at Neddy far below, making ready for another shot.

"*Hit,*" Neddy cried. Regret filled me. Here, come on over here, I'll tell you something, I wanted to say. You don't have to enjoy that kid's abuse or bend your head for him to throw things at for his fun. He doesn't matter, you don't need him. Your life will be easier, happier, more honest, more productive, than his. It's fated, you'll see.

I hadn't heard Leet. He must have left the wall and found Wayne and Neddy at the tree. Now he came around the house with a stamping walk, his head stuck forward and pointed up at Wayne in the tree, his arm flinging around in a motion of *get down here.* Neddy turned.

"You get down from there, you little bastard," Leet yelled. "What are you doing up there? Get down.

Was he throwing stuff at you? You'll get it now, boy. You never learn."

Leet stood at the foot of the tree, his hands on his hips, intent on Wayne above him. Neddy waited nearby, but off a little way from Leet. Leet stood. He went on yelling up at Wayne, who held his place for a moment, his legs spread apart among the branches, transfixed there by shafts of sunlight.

8

My LIFE on the SNOWPLOW

One boy I knew told how his father, when the boy went to him, said, "I don't want to hear this. Do you think I care? I don't care."

Other times his father would hammer their dinner table with his fist and shout hatred at his children.

"You, and you, and you, and *you!*" he'd shout. "I made you. I gave, gave. Why? For what? This? Look at you. God, I was free, *free!*"

At the end he would put his face in his hands and begin to weep, and later he'd be full of love, so they knew he was weak, but no less a mortal danger to them for that. The boy told me about it. He got out when he could. I don't care who you are or from where, what your condition of life. It's with you as it is with the first wildflowers that come out on our brown hillsides after the snow has gone: you have to push up through trash and hard thorns and a weight of old dead wood from other years, before you can feel the sun on your head.

How do I know? My father was never like my friend's. Well, my story is, he was a busy man, the busiest around, in fact. My father was a lawyer, and thirty years ago that gave him importance, or potential importance. Today there are more lawyers in Vermont than there are rabbits. Every little two-street town has lawyers by the dozen, and they are all busy. At the time I am telling of, lawyers were few among us, and those there were hadn't much to do, so they were apt to go into state politics. My father had been county prosecutor. He was one of the promising young men in the state. Good-looking, I suppose, and bright, and he could talk. At first I imagine him thinking, "I'll just see how far I can get." But soon he was in the game for good, and others in his party were talking about him for attorney general, for lieutenant governor. It was around this time that I got kicked out of Middlebury College.

I had begun my second year at Middlebury. One night I got drunk and had a fight with another student. I wound up with two broken fingers on my right hand. My opponent was unmarked. I'd swung at him, missed. Hit a door. I don't know how they feel at Middlebury today about drunken assault, but I know how they felt about it then: we were both expelled. In those days the college gave you a day to get out of town. I met with the dean in his office. He called my parents on the telephone. He spoke to my mother. Then he left the room, and I spoke to her. "Your father will have to drive over for you this afternoon or tonight," my mother said. "He probably doesn't have time," I said. "I can get the bus." "No," my mother said, "he wants to come."

But late that afternoon, when our car drove up to the dormitory where I had lived, she was driving, and my father wasn't with her. "He had to go to Bennington," she said. "He had the Republican Women's Club there. If you please. And so here am I. He said to tell you he'd see you late tonight. He's not angry," she said.

She was, though. It was plain from the way she drove the car when we started for home. I thought she was angry at me. "You can talk when he gets back," my mother said. She hardly spoke another word the whole way back to Ambrose.

He was late with the Republican Women that night, though, and stayed in Bennington. The day after, he had business at his office. So it wasn't until the next night that I saw my father. I came downstairs before dinner and found him in our front room. He'd taken off his suitcoat, but he wore his tie and waistcoat. He was pouring himself a whiskey. "I'd offer you one," he said, "but I see you can't handle it."

My father took his drink to the leather chair by the fireplace where he liked to sit. He set the glass carefully on the arm of the chair, then sat down himself. He picked up his drink, sipped it, looked at the whiskey in the glass, and finally looked at me.

"Who did you fight with?" he asked.

"Someone I was mad at. It wasn't a fight, really. We just sort of ran into each other."

"Where was he from?"

"Canada," I said. "Denny MacKinnon. Nobody you know. An asshole."

"I'd prefer you didn't talk like that at home," my father said. "I suppose he got fired too?"

"We both did," I said.

My father was trying to summon an appropriate measure of exasperation to direct at me. He leaned back in his big chair, putting his palms together judicially at his breast with his two index fingers playing under his chin. "Well, where were we?" he said. "Oh, yes. It looks like you've got a year off, doesn't it? Middlebury will have you back next fall, or I guess they will. You didn't kill him, did you? MacKinnon, I mean."

"No," I answered.

"That's good. Then they'll probably let you come back. Meantime, what are you going to do?"

One of my mother's brothers owned a ranch in Montana. I wouldn't have been the first in our family to pass through its purifying flame. My uncle always needed hands out there.

"I thought of going out to Paul's," I said. My father drank his drink. He made a face.

"I don't think so," he said. "What use have you for a bunch of damned cowboys, or they for you? Just because you disgraced yourself doesn't mean you get to waste a whole year playing ranch hand."

"All right," I said. "What do you want me to do? Stay here?"

My father looked up at me and tapped his index fingers together in front of his chin. Behind them he had begun to look sly.

"What do you say to working on the roads?" he asked. "You know, driving a plow with Arthur Tavistock's crew?"

"I don't know," I said. "Why not?"

"Why not, indeed," my father said. "I'll talk to Arthur."

So it was that I found myself living at home that winter for a season that was—what shall I say?—suspended, or partitioned off from my life before and after it. My parents hadn't expected to have me at home. They weren't prepared for me. My brother, Warren, who was seven years older than I, was not around. He had married in the summer just past, and that same fall he'd started at a law firm in Boston. Indeed, with being away at school and elsewhere, Warren hadn't lived at home much for ten years or more. Our house had forgotten him.

If I had wanted to be the child in the house again I could have had the place to myself. I didn't. At home now, it was as if I had been given new and better eyes and ears. I seemed to see and hear things I hadn't before. Ours was a quiet house, often empty. The clocks ticked through it. It was a sad house, I saw. The town was like the house. Ambrose was quiet, empty. It was just far enough back in the hills that nobody wanted to go anywhere, except for those who already had and wouldn't return. It had been that kind of town for a hundred years, but I saw it now for the first time. I was ready to light out for Montana, in spite of my father's judgment. I might have done it, too, but my father had talked to Arthur, and I was bound to a new rule, also discontinuous with my real life, but one that would serve us all for that season.

★ ★ ★

Arthur Tavistock was the road foreman in our town. He was a cousin of my father's, but he was older by ten or fifteen years. When I worked for him there were old people in Ambrose who called him Black Arthur, the name he'd had as a boy, to tell him from another Arthur in town at that time, Louisa Lamb's boy. Arthur Lamb was killed in Italy in 1944. He had been a pale-skinned blond—Light Arthur. Arthur Tavistock was the opposite of Light Arthur in color; his skin was brown, his hair black. He was a small, smart man with a line of sarcasm that was a little like my father's, although Arthur used his for command, to get you to do or believe something, while my father's sarcasm was to please himself. Arthur never puzzled me; my father, always.

Arthur had charge of the town road crew, at that time four men, and its equipment: three dump trucks for plowing snow, a light truck, and a garage full of snowplows, road rakes, rollers, ccment mixers, and tools. Arthur hired and fired the crew, decided what road, bridge, or culvert got fixed first, repaired the vehicles, and browbeat the selectmen for the money to keep the whole business running. The selectmen were content to put up with his know-all ways and his disrespect. They were content to refer to Arthur the townsman whose driveway had been washed away owing to a plugged culvert, or his neighbor whose car had slid into the snowbank and who wondered why his road was still always the last one to be cleared after each storm. Arthur always knew the reason. "We plow the school bus routes first. We'll get to you. You weren't going anywhere important, anyway."

"I'll talk to Arthur," my father said; not that he could have influenced Arthur to take me on, or that he would have tried. The road crew was apt to be short-handed in those days, particularly in the fall, as nobody wanted to plow snow. I went to the town garage one Monday morning in late October. Arthur was kneeling on the concrete floor before one of the trucks. He had several pieces of the truck's engine on the floor with him. "Hello there—Andrew," he said. "I saw your father the other day." Arthur looked over the parts spread before him, took one, and chipped at it with a little screwdriver. "Think you might like working on the roads, he said."

"I would."

"You were in college. Where did he say?"

"At Middlebury."

"Middlebury College. Had some trouble there, he said."

Don't make it too easy for him, I could imagine my father telling Arthur when they spoke. Go ahead and roast him a little bit if you want to. Make him squirm. I would not squirm.

"I was expelled," I told Arthur.

"Expelled. Got in a fight, your father said." Arthur got to his feet. He brushed off his knees, his bottom. "I never went to college," he said. "Can you drive?"

"I've never driven a truck."

"There's nothing to it," Arthur said. He stooped and picked up one of the engine parts from the floor, a steel casting the size of a dinner plate, with a heavy edge toothed to gear into something else.

"Know what this is?" he asked me.

"No," I said.

"Well, we aren't trying to say you'll be a mechanic," Arthur said. "Though it would have been nice."

★ ★ ★

Arthur set me to work cleaning up the garage that day, and all through the winter and into the spring, I never looked back. I was a road man, and that means a man with work to do. Road work in Vermont is a bit like farming in that every component of it looks forward or backward to one season; in farm work that season is harvest, and in road work it's winter. "This is a winter job all year around," Arthur said. "You're either getting through the winter, getting ready for winter, or patching up after."

Arthur got me started driving one of the big plow trucks. It was a six-wheel dump truck, and when I got up in the cab and sat behind the steering wheel, I was six or seven feet off the ground. I have to say I was afraid. Arthur climbed up with me. "Tricky, isn't it?" he said. "You're better off up here, you know. You can see everything, but if you should hit something, you'll probably be okay.

"Now, you can't really steer an outfit like this," Arthur said as we rolled out of the garage. "Just kind of point it and try to stay on the road. That's it. You're doing it."

The other three men on Arthur's crew were Win Anderson, Carl Pepper, and Norman Russ. Win and Carl were probably thirty and married. I never knew either of them well. Norman was younger, twenty-three or -four, and single. He was always talking about, working on, buying, or selling cars. In the summer he raced cars, he said. Arthur sometimes let Norman use an extra space in the town garage to work on them. Norman couldn't understand why Arthur wouldn't let him touch the trucks.

"Let me take that one for you, Arthur," Norman would say when Arthur was working under one of the big plow trucks.

"This is not a drag racer, Norman," Arthur said from under the truck. "We don't care how fast it goes or how much noise it makes. We don't care how much the little girls admire it. We just want you to bring it back alive. You aren't ready to work on this rig."

"Oh, hell, Arthur," said Norman.

"Get on up there and turn it over for me," Arthur said from beneath the great wheels.

The first snow fell on Thanksgiving Day. By Christmas time it lay a foot deep in the woods, and new storms came each week to add more. Arthur taught us to know the storms: dry northers and wet nor'easters. The northers came with a big wind driving the snow before the storm; the nor'easters were gentler snows that fell down through whole days, and in them, Arthur claimed, you could smell the sea.

He stood in the big door of the town garage on a gray afternoon, sniffing. "We work tonight," he said, "or tomorrow early."

Arthur worked into the night around the garage. He kept track of us, his crew. When the storms came, the equipment had to be running and the men had to be there.

"Nobody goes to Florida," Arthur said. "We work a regular week, but you have to stay close. It's part of the job. You hear on the radio that a storm is coming, or if you see one's coming, get on down here no matter where you are or what you're doing. Sunday or day off, I don't care—I can't go looking for you."

We obeyed. One night when my father was home, he invited me to go with him the next day to a luncheon in White River that he was speaking at. The next day was Saturday, and I didn't have to work. "I never see you," my father said. "Couldn't you use a break?"

The next morning I wondered if I should go. There was a yellow, shiny sky that looked like snow. The radio didn't say anything about a storm, however, and my father said, "Come on. We'll get you back in time if it starts to snow."

"It's too late if it's started and I'm not there," I said.

"I wish you'd come," my father said. So I did.

"How do you like road work?" my father asked me as we drove north.

"I like it all right."

"It's not a livelihood for you, though," he said.

"I don't know."

"I do. Will you be sorry to leave it in the spring, or whenever?"

"That's a long time away," I said.

"What do you think of Arthur?" my father asked me then.

"I don't know. I like him all right," I said.

"Arthur is a remarkable man. An able man. He could do so much more than what he does. But he never will. We tried to get him to run for selectman a few years ago. No soap. He wanted no part of it."

"He likes what he does, I guess," I said.

"Oh, sure he does," my father said. "But that's not enough for everybody. It can't be, or there is no reason for doing anything. You have got to stretch. Arthur's having a good time, but he's not stretching."

Well, I wasn't sure I wanted to listen to any more of that, and in any case the weather was looking worse. When we passed north of Springfield I could see a storm coming from behind Ascutney, and I could see the distant white commotion where it was snowing in New Hampshire. My father brought the car over when he saw it and stopped.

"I've got to get back," I said. "It's snowing over there right now."

"I guess you do," my father said. "But I can't take you all the way back now or I'll miss my engagement. I'm sorry. I never thought it would snow today. That's what I know about weather."

"I'll get a ride," I said. "Go on ahead."

"I don't like this."

I got out of the car and closed the door, but my father leaned over from the driver's seat and threw the door open again. Leaning across the seat he looked up at me from inside the car.

"Will you be all right?" he said.

"Oh, sure," I said.

"I don't like to maroon you."

"Well, what else can we do?" I said.

"Nothing," my father said. He closed the door, sat back up behind the wheel. He drove away.

I stood by the road for a minute, then started walking back the way we'd come. I could feel at my neck the damp air approaching with the snowstorm, but I saw no snow yet. In Ambrose, Arthur and the others would be gathering at the garage. They would be gassing the plow trucks.

I heard a car coming behind me, turned, and held out my thumb. No car appeared, though, and I realized that what I heard was the very loud engine of a car that was coming fast but was still some distance away. I waited. Then the car came around a bend, and I saw it. The driver must have been going eighty, and taking the bend had thrown him over to the wrong side of the road, but he never let up on the gas, and he came down on me in a blast of air like the storm that ran behind him. When he saw me he hit the brakes and nearly lost his rear wheels, which tried to slip around to one side. He went past me in a black wind, but finally he got stopped fifty yards farther down the road, then reversed and sped backward to pull up alongside me. He must be crazy, I thought. I won't ride with him.

The car was a big Fairlane, not new, with an engine which, even now that it was stopped, sounded as though it was about to jump out of the car, and a black paint job with orange flames on the front sides. The driver was Norman, pushing for home ahead of the storm just as I was, but making a good deal more speed.

"Jesus," Norman said, "did you see me? I was wide open. Did you hear it? Get on in," he said, "that old Arthur's going to be looking for us." I got in and shut the door, and Norman put the car in gear and stamped on the accelerator. The tires burned on the road, and we took off toward Ambrose. "Get set," Norman said. "We are going to challenge the sound barrier."

★ ★ ★

I didn't leave the town again that winter. My brother, Warren, came for Christmas with his new wife. He seemed very interested in me.

"You're working on the snowplows," he said. "Great! Outside work. Listen, don't let pa give you a bad time about it. It's the work you want to do, buddy, you do it. You're lucky."

Warren laughed, shook his head. "Isn't Arthur a card?" he said.

"Promise you'll come down and visit us soon," Warren's new wife said. "Promise me."

I stayed close. After the first of the year the storms seemed to follow one immediately upon the last, and often we worked around the clock. I'd come home to sleep for four or five hours, then make my way back to the garage, climb into a truck, plow, return to the garage for gas and to eat a sandwich, plow, sleep, plow.

The snow piled up. Arthur sat in a rocking chair beside an oil heater in one corner of the garage and looked out the door at the snows. As the winter went on he had less and less to say. We knew our jobs; talk had been for that. What was there to talk about now? Arthur rocked in his chair. None of us had much to say to the others. A day, two days, would pass for me with plowing, returning to the garage, going out again—and I'd realize I hadn't spoken a word to Arthur or to any of the other men, or they to me. We were dogged and silent as oppressed miners mining snow.

Even with the snow, my father was seldom home. He kept his meetings, speeches, dinners, going about in any weather.

"Carl pulled your father out of a snowbank last night," Arthur told me at the garage. "On the Pied Brook Road. He was trying to get to Brattleboro and the highway was closed, thought he'd go around that way. The snow was up under his bumper and he got so he couldn't see the road.

"I'd have thought he'd stayed home," Arthur said.

One night I came home as the moon was going down. There was a light in the window of my mother and father's room. I didn't have to go by there to get to where I slept. I let myself into the house as quietly as I could and started for the door to the back stairs, but I had to pass the front room, and when I did I looked in and saw my father sleeping on the sofa. He was wrapped in white sheets and blankets that the moonlight lay upon, and in the dark recess of the old sofa he shone. I hadn't meant to linger in the doorway, but I did, and my father abruptly sat up and said, "Who's that?"

"It's all right. It's me," I said. "What are you doing down here?" Before I finished saying it, I wished I hadn't.

"Well, your mother's not feeling right," my father said from the sofa. He must have been deeply asleep, for he was confused and his voice was changed. He put off some of his covers and set his feet on the floor. He turned on a light. The moonlight leapt back out the window onto the snow.

"The truth is, she's got her door locked," my father said. "Difficult times, Andrew," he said. He was shading his eyes against the light with his hand and looking at me.

I had come a little way into the room when he spoke to me. Now I stepped back into the hallway, meaning to shut the door after me.

"Stay," he said. "I'm awake now. Or is it late?"

"Late," I said. "It will be light in an hour."

"Has the storm quit? I rely on you for weather advisories now, you know. I don't pretend to understand it myself any more."

"It's quit," I said. "Goodnight. Shall I shut the door?"

"Sure," my father said. "She's sleeping." I closed the door.

I heard him turn the light out. She wasn't sleeping. I'd seen the light in their window before I came in the house, and when I went up the front stairs I could see the light under their bedroom door, and I could hear her in there.

★ ★ ★

I plowed through the night. Along the roads the snowbanks were six feet high, and during storms the lights of the truck lit the snowbanks and the snow that filled the air, so that I seemed to be driving through a white tunnel hung with curtains of the same white that parted endlessly before me. And although I was bucketing along through those tunnels in front of four or five tons of steel, and although the racket of the engine and of the plow grating on the frozen road beneath were frightful, the effect was of passing through a medium infinitely soft and silent. So much so that I can't say all of the things I saw along the roads as I drove the snowplow weren't dreams: deer that leaped miraculously across the road in front of the plow, owls that dipped in the air before my eyes on wide gray wings, and, one night, a man.

I was plowing on a road I don't know the name of in the far northeastern corner of Ambrose toward Dead River Settlement. Not many people lived that way. There were no more than three or four old farms on the road, and it had been a half hour since I'd passed the lights of a house. I was driving through woods. Behind the snowbank I could just see the big trees bending close. There was a man up ahead beside the road. He stood by the snowbank on the left side of the road with his hands in his pockets, looking up at the plow as it approached. He looked small and young, my age or a little older. He was in white, or some pale color, and I don't think he had any coat, but I can't be sure. Certainly he had no hat. His hair was blond.

He didn't wave or make any other sign, or even move. I slowed to pass him. I was a little frightened of him all by himself out there in the middle of the woods in a blizzard without a coat, and I wasn't about to stop unless he made some sign of distress. I went by him, and as I did he bowed his head so I couldn't see his face, just his pale head.

I left him behind then, but no more than half a mile down the road I found a car coming toward me. It was coming too fast, slipping all over the road, throwing sprays of snow to the side. I steered the plow well over to the right and stopped, but the other car, instead of going by, braked hard, locked its wheels, and skidded to a stop a few feet ahead, nearly fetching into the plow. Nobody got out of the car. I didn't know what to do. At last I got down and went over. The driver's window opened, releasing a rush of heated air that smelled as though it came right off the saloon floor. Inside, a fat figure in an overcoat, wearing a baseball cap. It was Wilson Nye, having drunked-up at his favorite tavern out on the highway, now trying to navigate himself back to his home past Dead River and making a heavy job of it.

Wilson opened the door and got out of the car. His cap was on backward, the brim pointing behind, the way somebody had clapped it onto Wilson's head as they shoved him out the door of the Riverbend at closing time. Wilson was carrying on about something.

"My God," he said. "I hit a man. Where the Christ is he? It was back there," he pointed down the road in the direction I'd come from. "I never saw him before I hit him," Wilson said. "I didn't even know what happened. Went on. Then I turned around up ahead and came back. Where is he? What am I going to do?"

"I saw him," I said. "You didn't hit him. He was all right."

"I had to hit him," Wilson cried. "I saw him thrown, I heard him hit. Before I knew it I was past him, then I turned around up there and came back. We've got to find him. He'll freeze if he isn't dead."

"I'm telling you," I said. "I saw him. He was standing by the road."

Wilson had to go back and look, though, so I pulled the plow off the road into a turnaround that was near and shut it off, and Wilson and I went back down the road in his car. I drove. There was nobody at the place where I had seen the pale man. We drove slowly. We stopped the car and got out so Wilson could look over the snowbanks. We couldn't see his car's tracks in the snow, since I'd come this way with the plow behind him.

"I know I hit him," Wilson said. "I've had some drinks, though."

Wilson was not in good shape. He was shivering now, and he could just walk. I thought I'd better drive him home. His place was a couple of miles from where we were. I got the car turned around and started off. Wilson had gone to sleep. When we drove up to his house, a light went on in one of the windows, and Wilson's wife came out putting on a coat. She was a lean woman with a big jaw and the look of one who handled things well without making a fuss. Together we piled Wilson into the house and sat him in the kitchen. He'd waked up. "That's the goddamnedest thing I ever saw," he was saying. He was still thinking about the man he believed he'd run over. He wanted to tell his wife about it. She wasn't interested.

Wilson's wife thought I had been out drinking with Wilson. "We thank you for helping him home," she said. "Take his car back with you."

"I can walk," I said.

"Take the car," she said. "Go on. He's not going anyplace. He can walk for it tomorrow morning himself. It will clear his head."

"I will. Thank you," I said. I left them and drove Wilson's car back to the turnaround where I'd parked the plow.

I never told anyone about the man I saw by the road. In the end I'd decided he was a dream, and at that time I hadn't anyone I told my dreams to. I never told about the little adventure with Wilson Nye, either. I'd broken a rule to help him that night. Arthur forbade us ever to stop and leave the plows, except in an emergency, and he wouldn't have accepted Wilson Nye driving home blind drunk as an emergency.

Months later I was picking up some lumber at a sawmill in Ambrose. Wilson worked at the mill, and when he saw me in the yard he came out of the shed and walked over. I hadn't seen him since the night in the woods, but he started in on the man he'd run over as though we'd been arguing about him an hour before. "If that wasn't somebody I hit," he said, "then maybe you can tell me what it was."

"I can't say," I told Wilson.

"I'll tell you what," Wilson said. "It was a deer." He removed his baseball cap and wiped his forehead with his arm. "It was a deer," he said again. "It had to been."

What I saw was no deer. Maybe it was a dream and maybe it wasn't, but in either case I hold it was no deer. It was, then and now, a young man or boy whom I'd never seen before, towheaded, no coat, no hat, so cold, two miles from the nearest house on a bad night. Wilson Nye may have hit a deer; but my fellow was different—a little dream man or a little ghost who hadn't parents any more to make him button up.

I don't remember just what day it was when I saw him, but it was near the time when winter began to let go. There came a week, then two weeks, with no storms. The snow began to go down, and the mud came up in the roads. It splashed on the snowbanks, and they went down more quickly. March Meeting came. Arthur got up in front of the selectmen and the assembled townspeople and spoke in praise of the job the road crew had done over a hard winter. He asked for an expression of gratitude. He got it. He asked for a twenty percent increase in the road budget. He got five.

We were scraping and filling muddy roads, working daylight hours. Then an April snow came, with two feet falling over a day and two nights. We put on the plows again. But in April you know winter can't win as long as the solar system stays on the tracks, and we believed we had come through it. The sun came in the doors of the town garage. Arthur had moved his rocking chair from beside the heater and set it in the doorway. He was talking again.

"We made it through another one," he said. "It's over now. Fishing pretty soon. Everybody gets a vacation. That's instead of a bonus. I tried to talk the selectmen into a bonus for the road crew, but they wouldn't have it. They never do. Next winter maybe they'd like to shovel the roads instead of us plow them."

★ ★ ★

We finished work at three in the afternoon. Some days Norman and I would drive around for an hour or two after work. Norman would buy us beer, and we'd drink it while we drove. Then he'd leave me off at home. Norman always drove. "You ought to get a car," he said. "I know a man who's got something he wants to sell. Bel Air. Fifty-two. He wants four hundred but I could get it for you for two or two-fifty because it needs a new clutch. I could do that work for you. It's a good car. It goes."

"I don't want a car," I said. "Besides, I don't have two hundred for it."

"Christ, Andrew," Norman said, "you must have it. You get paid, don't you? I know you never buy anything. You never go anywhere. God, I'm surprised you don't spit nickels and dimes every time you open your mouth to talk. Now I'm telling you about a nice vehicle that will take you where you want to go, and you're telling me you don't have two hundred dollars. You're too young to be so cheap, Andrew. We both are."

"I'm saving up," I said. It was true. I was banking my pay, and my father observed it, too. One afternoon Norman and I drove up to our house to let me out, and my father was on the front porch. I went up the walk and up the steps to join him there, and Norman drove off with a blast of his engine and a loud burning of tires.

"That kid is a jerk," my father said.

"He has a car he wants me to buy," I said.

"Like his?"

"I guess so."

"You have money, anyway," my father said.

"I'm not getting a car," I said. "I'll need the money for school."

"Ah," my father said. "You plan to go back to Middlebury for next year, is that right?"

"Yes. I'm going back," I said.

"I'm glad," he said. "You have worked hard this winter. I've never worked as you have, on the roads with the plowing and so on. I bet you enjoyed it."

"I did."

"You'd have to have," my father said. "But you have done it now, and I'm glad you're not going to pretend it's a real life for you."

"You think Arthur pretends that?" I said.

"Not for a minute," my father said. "Arthur doesn't pretend anything, any more than I do."

There is no doubt my father liked the sound of his own voice, and if I may put it this way, the sound of his own ideas, of his own predicament. He and Arthur were alike in that way. He'd been trying all winter to get me to say I'd return to school, and now I'd said it. My secret was that I hadn't ever had any other purpose. I couldn't stay home, not then. I couldn't stay in a place that required me to live in an unhappy house, to learn what it was that made it unhappy, to sound the bottom of unhappiness and likely be claimed by it myself. No. I had to get on.

From our porch my father looked down the street along the last dirty snowbanks on either side to where the street went around a corner past somebody's barn and became again a country road that led among the wooded hillsides, where the rotten, warm snow lay in patches still, and would right into May. "Spring," he said.

"I don't know," my father said. "It seems as if you go on all winter, and then it's when spring comes that you feel old."

"I know," I said.

"You don't," my father said. "How could you?"

9

CRIME
of the
CENTURY

I was driving to White River. Johnson used to buy machinery in White River years ago, but I never go there any more except to visit Orson Bland, who was county sheriff when I was young and who is now living in the Veterans Administration Hospital at White River. Orson won't be coming out of the hospital, so I go up there every couple of months to see him.

Five miles out of White River I passed a hitchhiker waiting beside the road. After I'd gone on by him I realized it was Kevin, who was one of the hired men around Johnson's place twenty years ago. I don't know that I would have recognized Kevin if it hadn't been Orson, the sheriff, I was on my way to see. Orson and Kevin had never met, but that wasn't Orson's fault, for Kevin was in his line of work: a thief and a fugitive. He was supposed to have made off with a fancy coat of Johnson's when he left Johnson's employ. Johnson reacted to that minor theft as though it was a triple axe murder. For weeks he tormented Orson, who Johnson felt wasn't working hard enough at tracking Kevin down. Nobody ever proved Kevin stole Johnson's coat; all that was for sure was that the coat was gone and so was Kevin, Johnson's no-good farmhand.

Now, twenty years later, here Kevin was, traveling by thumb, northbound. He had a pack on his back, like any kid, and he held his right arm out, thumbing for cars that didn't stop. In his free hand he held a square of brown cardboard with where he was going printed on it in green letters large enough for me to read as I went past.

I hadn't recognized Kevin in time to stop for him. A hundred feet beyond where he stood I tried to slow down and get over so I could go back. There was no shoulder to pull onto, though, and when I slowed, a log truck the size of a small mountain bore down on me, the driver blasting his air horn and making his brakes hiss and spit. I looked in the rearview, and there he was, about six inches from my back end: BIG JOHN. A lot of those log trucks have names or mottoes painted on the radiator. This truck's name was Big John, and he was letting me know he could roll right over me and never feel the crunch. I tried to speed up and was cranking down my window so as to make a rude and unmistakable gesture to the logger when he swung out and passed me like a hurricane, leaving at most half an inch between my frail craft and his towering load of logs.

By the time I got off the road and stopped, Kevin was gone. Somebody must have picked him up while the log truck was chasing me. I wondered if Kevin had seen the logger run me down. He'd been a logger up north, or anyway he used to say he had, and he loved those great, menacing trucks.

Kevin came from one of the logging towns back of St. Johnsbury. He was middle-sized or short, with long arms and a low waist. Johnson used to say Kevin left the north country because the only jobs there were logging jobs, and all the logging jobs seemed too much like real work to Kevin, with the exception of driving one of those big trucks—and for that job he was unsuited because he couldn't see over the steering wheel. Johnson liked to leave the implication that Kevin was no good to him.

One of Johnson's difficulties with Kevin, and with other of the younger hands, was that the men he hired expected to be workers and were happy to be workers, while Johnson was unhappy at finding they weren't serfs.

"It used to be," Johnson said, "you'd hire a man and he'd stay. He'd work on the same place all his life. He'd know your place as well as you. Better. You and the hired man would be more like partners—well, almost—than like a boss and a man. Now, hell, you can't get anything but these kids. They don't stay. They don't save their wages. They have to have cars, radios, the TV, vacation time. Then they quit in two months and go someplace else. Nobody wants to stay and do a job any more."

Johnson liked a man who knew his way around a farm and who wanted to see things set right. He liked, in the morning, to give his man the job of dressing a field and to have the man say, well, if the fence around such and such a pasture isn't mended today it won't hold the cows when they come out. Then Johnson would have that man mend the fence before he started the field.

A kind of delicacy was missing in the way Kevin did what Johnson directed him to do. He did it, usually well and in good time; but he didn't show any thought or purpose for it.

"You want to get the spreader and start on that field," Johnson would say.

"Sure," Kevin said.

"Unless there is something else you saw or didn't get done yesterday."

"I guess not."

"Well," Johnson said, "what about that fence? Isn't it pretty bad?"

"It seems like it is."

"Maybe you better work on that fence today, then."

"Sure," Kevin said.

"Well, what do you think about it?" Johnson would ask.

"To be truthful with you, I don't care one way or another," Kevin said.

★ ★ ★

That kid, Johnson thought, never bought that thing with any wages he got from me.

He regarded Kevin's new car, which Kevin had taken to parking in the yard. Kevin had driven up in the car several days before. He drove off in it every evening after he finished his work, returning late. The car was used but not old.

Since Kevin had driven up in that car, Johnson had been a worried man. No hired man of Johnson's had ever owned a car, at least not while he worked for Johnson. The fact that Kevin could buy and keep a car meant he had some source of income other than the wages Johnson paid him. What would that be? Johnson thought he knew. He was fairly certain Kevin wasn't out selling encyclopedias on his time off. But nothing was missing from around the place. And when Johnson watched the papers and asked around, he found nobody who had been held up, looted, or swindled. Johnson went on worrying.

Kevin must never know Johnson's worry over him. Therefore Johnson was stuck. To satisfy himself that Kevin was harmless, Johnson would have to watch him, question him, and, sooner or later, alert him to his suspicions. On the other hand, supposing Kevin was what Johnson thought he was, Johnson's only protection would be in getting rid of Kevin for no good reason. Either way he betrayed weakness. Johnson could only settle the issue of Kevin by acting the part of an anxious ruler who from doubt of his own authority must banish, of all his subjects, his strongest liege.

Some of the men Johnson had hired over the years he could joke along in a situation like this; Kevin wasn't one of them. Where did you steal that rig, Rolly? Johnson could have said. Might Kevin tell him if he asked?

"That's quite a car of yours," he said one evening as Kevin was setting out.

"It burns oil," Kevin said.

"You ought to have somebody look at it, then," Johnson said.

"It isn't worth it to me to put anything into it that way," Kevin told him.

Not worth it to him, thought Johnson.

Johnson always spoke of Kevin, and of Kevin's fellows around the place, as if they were youths. "Let the kid do it," Johnson would say, or, "I'll get the kid to take care of it." In fact Kevin must have been in his early thirties when he worked for Johnson. He was no kid: Johnson paid him in real money. Had Kevin been a kid, Johnson would have paid him nothing, which is what he paid me. I was the kid around Johnson's, not Kevin.

I was encouraged in the summers to go about with the hired men around Johnson's place and be whatever help I could to them. Somebody must have expected I'd learn something useful. I did learn things from Johnson's hands, some of them useful, some of them things my mother probably would not have gotten around to teaching me. From one of the hands I learned how to roll a cigarette, from another I learned seventeen verses to "If All the Young Ladies." Kevin's instruction was less pointed. From him I learned to keep clear of log trucks.

Kevin was not talkative. Many of the hired men, especially the older ones, were. They liked to talk as they worked. Kevin stuck silently to his work for the most part, perhaps because he never expected, as the old men did, that his working time could be anything but burdensome. If Kevin and I were at a job, the only talk that would pass between us would be his directions to me. If we rested, he would sit looking at his feet or at nothing. Only on the topic of log trucks did Kevin ever have much to say.

We had been cutting brush from around a fence that ran along the road. We were resting. A logger came down the road, loaded up and making speed. We watched him pass.

"Look at that mad bastard," Kevin said.

"Who's that?" I asked him.

"That driver. He was loaded four feet too high, he was doing sixty or sixty-five, and he was rocking. If he'd have run over a garter snake he'd have flipped. They're top heavy. All the loggers are. They are only supposed to load the trucks just so high or they'll tip over, like on a curve. The regulations say, load—I don't know—ten or eleven feet high. But hell, they have to move the logs. That's what they get paid for. Nobody pays any attention to the regulations. They stack them up there until the truck can't move any more, then they take off one log and send the driver on his way. Most of the time they make it all right. But a few times one will flip over, and when that happens you don't want to be underneath. I had a cousin. . . . Of course the driver is a dead man, too, but those guys just don't care. They are crazy, and they love that work. The worse the road is, the worse the weather, the better they like it. It's like being in a war."

"What about your cousin?" I asked Kevin.

"Who?" he asked.

"You said you had a cousin. Was he a driver?"

"Oh. No. He worked in the cheese factory. He was just driving along. A logger was coming the other direction. They went past each other on a bad curve. The logger flipped over on my cousin."

"Was he killed?" I asked.

"You bet," Kevin said. "Where I used to live," he said, "a good many still use horses for logging. They take the logs out of the woods in the winter on a big sled with a team."

"That's a better way, I guess," I said.

"I guess," Kevin said. "It's safer, anyhow. Still, being truthful with you, the only ones using horses are those that can't afford a truck, which is almost everybody around there. Being a logger is the best way I know about to stay poor."

★ ★ ★

Johnson had been in Brattleboro. He reached home at half past four in the afternoon and drove into the yard. There was some commotion by the barn. He drove over there. The cattle were milling about before the gate that let into the barn enclosure. Someone should have brought them in an hour ago. Kevin should have. Johnson was still in his car. He looked back across the yard toward the house. Kevin's car was in the yard, and the front door of the house was standing open. Johnson thought of reversing and driving off for help. That would leave the cows still untended to. He got out of his car, went to the gate, and let the cows in. Then he crossed the yard to the house.

Someone had been over the place. Still, when he got done counting the spoons, Johnson found that nothing was missing except a coat. He had assumed that Kevin, seeing his opportunity, would bring in a band of henchmen with a truck and pick the place clean to the pictures on the walls. Instead, Johnson's coat was all that had been taken.

Was Kevin the thief? Johnson thought so. Why, then, had he left his car behind? Johnson thought— because Kevin knew the car would be reported and watched out for—the car was a risk for him now. Still, without the car Kevin would be taking a greater risk.

He'd be walking through country where everyone who
passed knew who he was and where he came from, and
he'd be wearing Johnson's fancy coat.

Johnson didn't care. If Kevin was not the thief,
then some unknown second person must be supposed
to have happened on Johnson's place when Johnson was
away and Kevin was unaccountably missing, and to have
surveyed the place, entered, taken, and left. For months
Johnson had worried about Kevin's intentions. Now
what he had feared for so long had come to pass, and he
was asked to believe that the culprit was some un-
foreseen, inconceivable drifter, who fitted into the complex machine of his suspicions about Kevin like a key in
a lock, but was not Kevin. No.

If Kevin was innocent, why had he disappeared?

It was the coat that Johnson missed, whose loss
wouldn't go away. It was the coat, the thought of which
in the days after the theft drove him from his chair and
sent him about the house from one window to another.
The coat gone, and the coat having been lifted from its
hook in the upper hallway of Johnson's house by Kevin,
who had entered, opened every door, looked in every
room, taking his time, alone in Johnson's house while
Johnson was away.

It was a hunting coat, new. Johnson had never
even worn it out of doors. The coat was tan with a
brown corduroy lining to the collar and a corduroy
patch on the right shoulder where you set the stock of
your bird gun. It was fitted with loops at the left breast
for keeping shells, and a large pocket was sewn on the
skirt behind to hold the birds you shot.

Three or four days after the robbery Johnson
became convinced that nobody was doing anything

about it. He went to Orson Bland, the county sheriff. The story he got there was that Orson and his men had called at houses around Johnson's asking if Kevin or any stranger had been seen on the day of the robbery. Nobody had seen anything. What more were they doing, Johnson wanted to know? "Well," Orson told him, "nothing."

There wasn't much more they could do in a case like this, Orson explained. Johnson wouldn't take that. Hadn't they ever heard of stolen-property traces, of alerts for suspected persons? What about canvassing the second-hand stores? Had they done that? What about known dealers in stolen goods in southern Vermont and adjacent states? Had they interrogated them?

"For a coat?" Orson said. "Look, Clark," he told Johnson, "our office is me and three deputies, one part-time. I can't pull everybody off other jobs because somebody swiped your coat. We have got drunk drivers, assaults, accidents, writs; and every one of them is more important than your damned coat—which anyway got stolen last week, and crime marches on, like they say."

"What about the state police?" Johnson asked. "Do they do their job any more?"

"The state police know all about your coat, Clark, and they know all about the kid," Orson told him. "And they are a lot less likely to find it or him than we are." He leaned back in his chair. "Buy yourself another coat and forget about it," Orson said, but Johnson just shook his head, disgusted.

"And if you don't like the way this office conducts its business," Orson told him, "you can vote Democratic next year."

The following day Johnson was back. He began
by being reasonable. It was not reasonable, he said, to
suppose that Kevin had simply vanished.

"Here's a kid who looks like a jailbird anyway,"
Johnson said, "walking the roads in a coat that's seventy-
five bucks from Abercrombie & Fitch. People have got
to have seen him, remembered him, and you'd find them
if you'd look. But you aren't looking. I don't know what
I've been paying taxes for all these years, do you?"

"We have done all we can," Orson told Johnson.
"We have done in your case just the way we have done
in every other case. You don't like the outcome. There
isn't any outcome. There seldom is. And anyway, if there
were, there's no criminal case here. If that kid were to
walk into this office this minute, there is nothing we
could do but ask him politely if he knows anything
about a coat that disappeared from your place the other
day.

"It is finished, for everyone but you," Orson said.
"It's a petty theft, Clark. Nobody's killed, nobody's hurt.
Forget about it. And forget that you are an indignant
citizen. Nobody has let you down except what's his
name—Kevin. And for all you really know, he hasn't,
either."

Johnson hit the sheriff's desk with his fist so that
the papers on it jumped.

"God damn it," he said. "He stole my coat."

★ ★ ★

At the VA Hospital in White River I left my car in the lot
and went up to the floor where Orson was. There is a

sunroom on his floor that gets the afternoon light, and Orson was out there. He has a tomato plant he keeps in a pot in the sunroom, and he was picking off sucker shoots. Orson is in a wheelchair. I gave him a can of tobacco I had brought, and he held it in his lap.

I told Orson about seeing Kevin on the road on my way in. I had to remind him who Kevin was.

"Oh, sure," Orson said. "The fellow Clark said stole his good clothes, was it, or something? His coat, wasn't it—his hunting coat? Poor Clark."

Orson looked out the window to the west, where the hills went off into the distance, hill after hill, green, then blue, then gray.

"Where do you suppose he was going?" he asked.

I haven't any idea, I almost said, when I thought, sure, I do. I knew where Kevin was going. He had held that sign, a piece of cardboard with where he was going printed on it in green letters. I had read it as I went by, and so I answered Orson.

"St. Johnsbury."

10

The EXILE, the HOUSEKEEPER, and FLORA, the BEAUTY of ROME

Over here you have nothing to fear from any policeman if you have a valid driver's license. If you're sober and have a valid driver's license. If you're something else, and sober, and have a valid driver's license. White.

Tyzack did not open his eyes. Earlier the voice of his benefactor had seemed to lull him. The walls of his room stood in shadow, brightening. He looked about, but then he shut his eyes again, allowed himself to become involved again in sleep, not for long, he knew. Hilde, grown, was reading to him. She sat at a window. The light fell on the page in her lap, her face in shadow. Tyzack listened. Someone was always reading, in a soft voice or silently. There was a noise of car tires on a

gravel drive, his drive, and an engine started. At the
noise, he thought Hilde looked up from her book.

Tyzack raised himself on his elbow and turned
himself to the window by his bed. His house was still
dark from the trees around it, but farther down the hill
the light entered his meadow by irregular salients of
yellow. At the end of the meadow Wright's house was in
daylight. While Tyzack watched, the light crossed the
lawn and came toward him at the window. He felt chill
on his shoulders.

He heard the side door open, heard Anne enter
the kitchen, put her things down by the kitchen door.
He heard her at the stove remove the lids, put in paper
and sticks. She wouldn't take care to be quiet, knowing
he was awake in there. Tyzack sat up, put his feet on the
floor.

★ ★ ★

In the kitchen Anne lit the fire. She took off her coat and
hung it on its hook. At the sink she ran water into the
kettle, took it to the stove. A little smoke rose from the
cracks around the stove lids. Anne sneezed. She listened
for Tyzack, heard his chair creak as he lowered his
weight into it, and heard him roll across the uneven
floor into his bathroom. Mornings at this point Anne felt
useless and wondered if she ought not to go back to her
own home. She put a plate of buns in the center of the
table, with butter on a dish and a clean coffee cup. She
laid her hand on the top of the stove and felt it warming
under the kettle.

Anne left the kitchen by the back door. She went
through the woodshed, and so outside. The grass was
wet. It wet her shoes and ankles.

She was thirty-two, the youngest of five, and the only girl. Ages were important in her life, the differing ages of people. Her husband, Harold Tavistock, was nearly twenty years older than she. The difference in their ages had pleased Anne during their courtship. It still pleased her. But also age parted Anne and Harold, it put between them a distance fixed while they both lived. The difference in their ages was like a long ladder they carried together, one at each end. It kept them together, and it kept them apart. Harold grew tired. He worked hard. In the evening he fell asleep in his chair.

Around the house flowers grew beneath the windows where Anne walked. The taller flowers were bent down to the grass with their own weight and with the weight of the dew. By the end of summer the high phlox, hollyhocks and others had grown too tall. They fell over at the root and lay about. Anne would tie them to stakes, if she had the time, to give them a couple of more weeks until the heavy frosts finished them. Across the lawn in the unmown grass the autumn roadside flowers, goldenrod and aster, now bloomed. The light had reached them in the meadow, Anne saw, and they held the light. She went back to the house.

Tyzack was sitting at the kitchen table. He had not begun to eat, for he waited until she came in.

"Good morning, Mrs. Tavistock," he said.

"Good morning," Anne said. She put a cup of coffee by him.

"Ah, thank you," Tyzack said. He picked up the coffee cup, drank. "Excellent," he said.

"We had a call from Hugh last night," Anne said. Hugh was her brother.

"Oh?"

"Yes. He's coming down this afternoon. He'll stop, but he didn't know when he'd get here."

Tyzack finished his coffee and Anne went to get him more.

"He's bringing a book for you," Anne said. She put Tyzack's second cup of coffee down before him.

"Did he say what book?"

"He didn't say," Anne said.

"Well, it's good of him." Tyzack took his coffee cup in his lap and rolled back from the table. He would go into the sitting room, and Anne would make his bed and straighten his room.

"I ought to fill the woodboxes when your room is finished," she said. "Would you like to come out back in a while?"

"Sure," Tyzack nodded. "You say when you're ready." He rolled into the other room.

Tyzack drew himself up beside the window. He set his coffee on the sill. Coming in from the kitchen with the cup in his lap he had spilled no coffee. When Tyzack's bones began to crumble, Anne's brother, Hugh, went over the first floor of Tyzack's house with a claw hammer, taking up all the door sills. The essence of being a goddamned invalid, Tyzack thought, is preparation—order and preparation.

Outside the window, the road passed his house in a curve as it started down the hill. Across the road the hill went down through a meadow to woods. At the end of the meadow was Tyzack's neighbors' house, just inside the trees.

Tyzack's neighbors were Wrights: father, mother, and four sons, nearly grown. The father seemed to Tyzack no older than the boys.

The yard of their house was full of old cars, and

several other cars were disposed about the end of the meadow nearby. Wrights were forever working on these cars, but none of the cars ever ran, or ever drove away. That puzzled Tyzack until it came to him that the Wrights were not trying to repair the cars. They were taking parts from them to repair other cars. When one had no useful parts left they shoved it out in the meadow. Tyzack was pleased. It was a source of satisfaction that he had penetrated to the intention of the people among whom he seemed to be passing his final years of life.

Tyzack said that he had spent the first third of his life studying, the next third running. The last third he would spend sitting at a window looking out at a near-wilderness peopled by North Americans: the same fate as that of more than a few principled men who had tried to move the European democracies into the middle of the present century by orderly means, and failed, as everyone knows.

Anne came in. "Are you ready?" she asked.

"Sure," Tyzack said, "if you are." He turned his chair from the window so Anne could get behind. She took hold of the back of his chair and pushed him to the kitchen door, opened it, and rolled him over the sill, throwing her weight back to ease the bump to the step outside. She pushed his chair through the woodshed and into the sun.

"How's that?" she asked.

"That's good," Tyzack said.

Anne went back into the house and came out with the wood barrel from the sitting room. It was a metal tub, half again as big as a bushel basket. She set it down inside near the chopping block.

Tyzack sat with the sun at his back, facing the

woodshed. He twisted about in his chair and looked for
the sun. It stood clear of the trees, halfway up the sky,
though the house still threw a shadow that now fell
across Tyzack's knees. The sun burned his eyes, but it
didn't warm him. It was a winter sun even now.

It was the changing angle of the sun reaching the
Earth's northern and southern hemispheres that
accounted for the seasons, a minute shift on the scale of
the heavens, but nevertheless one that told in every cell
of Tyzack, who could feel the degree of difference between the summer sun of ten o'clock on an August
morning and the diminished sun of the same hour in the
next month.

At one time in his life Tyzack had taught French
at a school in England. One of the science masters there
had an orrery. It was an affair of cranks, rods, and gears
that represented the motions of the planets around the
sun; not all the planets: Venus, Earth, Mars and Jupiter
only. When you turned the crank that worked the Earth,
a ball the size of a pea revolved around a fixed ball the
size of a tennis ball, painted yellow, that represented the
sun. The Earth's gears were arranged so that it sped
around, though you tried to turn the crank slowly.
When you turned the crank for Jupiter, a ball the size of
a large cherry revolved slowly and could not be made to
hurry.

Tyzack admired the science master's orrery. He
could recall its color and motion even when England
had otherwise grown dim in his memory. He thought of
it when the seasons changed. The orrery seemed to
confirm changes that his own body too detected.

The sunlight had entered the woodshed. It fell
on Anne's legs as she worked at the chopping block, but

her arms and upper body were in the dark. She was splitting large round blocks from a pile at her feet. She split each round in two, then each half, then two of the quarters. That done, she put down the axe and placed the six splits upright in the wood bucket. Then she set a fresh round on the block and began again with the axe.

Anne was a strong and practiced axeman. She didn't expect to part the wood without hitting it hard. Often Tyzack heard the axe ring as the wood split clean in one stroke. Still, Anne didn't swing the axe as a man would. Tyzack had thought about men and women using each other's tools. Anne held the axe out, away from her body; a man would have held it closer, more familiarly. And, Tyzack knew, Anne didn't give herself to the work of wood splitting as a man would have. This morning she would split what she needed to fill the boxes, and then she would quit. A man—Anne's brother, Hugh, for instance, or Harold—would give himself to the rhythm and mystery of the work and go on until there was nothing left to split. Hugh or Harold would excel Anne at splitting, though she was stronger than either of them now and had a better eye for the work.

The wood barrel was full. Anne put down the axe, picked up the barrel by its handle, and carried it to where Tyzack sat by the woodshed door. "Can I get you anything?" she asked.

"Nothing," Tyzack said.

Anne picked up the barrel again and started into the house. The barrel was awkward to carry, and she bumped it with her hip; but she lifted it without much trouble. Full of wood, it would weigh seventy-five pounds.

Inside, Anne put the wood down in the sitting room, and then went to the kitchen and ran a glass of water in the sink. Out the windows in the yard, Tyzack sat in the sun. Anne drank. She had not liked the idea of coming to Tyzack's as housekeeper for an invalid. She had found, though, that Tyzack took care of himself. The kind of care of his person that she had expected wasn't up to her. She was past minding if women she knew in the village told newcomers, or people Anne hadn't met, that she did housecleaning. Harold might not like the arrangement, but he didn't say anything. If she weren't up at Tyzack's house she would be working in a store, or home alone all day.

What Anne feared was that one day she would come in to Tyzack or arrive in the morning to find him dead. As long as she went on working for him, Anne knew, she could be certain that day would come. There was no one else who would find him.

Hugh had let the town of Ambrose know years ago that Tyzack was in history's reckoning their most distinguished resident, that he was a larger figure by far than the former governor of the state who also lived among them. Nobody in Ambrose knew or cared to contradict Hugh's appraisal of Tyzack's stature. And so they accepted it, accommodated Tyzack, and accommodated Anne, their sister, as the woman who looked after him.

Anne put her water glass in the sink. She got the kitchen woodbox from beside the stove and took it out to the woodshed, where she began splitting blocks again. Tyzack had turned his chair so the sunlight hit his profile. He was looking away up the long hill above the house toward the pasture at the top that belonged to Clark's house. The sun flashed off his glasses.

The order of their day was that Anne and Tyzack converged, parted, converged. In the morning they kept each other company. They got onto some curious subjects together. A new doctor had come to the town some time ago, a woman. Tyzack had asked Anne about her. Anne said she wouldn't go to that doctor. She wouldn't want a woman going over her as a doctor, she said. Tyzack said his daughter was a doctor, in New York.

Anne knew of Tyzack's daughter from her brother but knew nothing about her. She imagined Tyzack's daughter lived overseas or was lost. Anne wondered, if the daughter lived as near as New York, why she never visited Tyzack. "She would, certainly," Tyzack said, "if she knew I was here."

Anne put the axe away. She took a stool to the outside door of the shed and sat for a moment with Tyzack. He turned his chair about toward her. She was warm with working on the firewood, and around her face some of the hair was damp and stuck against the skin at her temples. She pushed it back with her fingers. She looked at Tyzack in his chair, shading her eyes with her hand.

"How do you feel?" Anne asked.

"Good," Tyzack said.

"Are you warm?"

"Sure. Sit down," he said.

"For a minute," Anne said.

"How is the wood?" Tyzack asked her.

"How is it? It's all right," Anne said. "You should have more. I could get Harold or one of the others to bring up another load."

"I talked to Tom the other day," Tyzack said. "He'll be bringing some more whenever he can get it."

"That's good," Anne said. She stood, picked up the woodbox, and went with it into the house. Tyzack turned back to the hillside. The sun fell right down upon the slope in a benign confusion of light that seemed to arrive on the open hillside as motion as well as light, stirring above the warm grass like bees.

When Anne came back out she carried two cups of coffee. She handed one to Tyzack and sat down again on her stool in the shed door. She drank her coffee. But Tyzack still held his cup as he had taken it from her. Anne looked at the corner of the house where the fallen-over flowers lay. "I'll stake up the flowers after lunch," she said. After a moment Tyzack turned to her. "What did you say, Mrs. Tavistock?" he asked.

Anne didn't answer him. She was still looking toward the flowers by the house. There, around the corner, a brown animal had come quickly toward them that Anne had taken for an injured puppy from its strange way of creeping, until she saw it was a large rabbit. It came right in to them, and Anne expected it to see them and shy away, but the rabbit stopped within a few feet of where they sat and turned its side to them, holding still in the grass. Tyzack had seen it too now. The rabbit did not fear them, Anne saw, but had come in to them with some purpose. She looked at the rabbit: close, large, its color the brown of dead fern.

"What is it doing?" Tyzack asked.

Anne shook her head. Before them the rabbit gathered its legs under it and settled into the grass, its delicate ears low, its hindquarters humped, its calm black eye set in a look oblique, cast down and back, attentive. Its eye was still.

Anne watched it. In the grass bright with the

sun, the rabbit was dark; it had brought the thicket's darkness with it out onto the open lawn.

She had scarcely seen a live rabbit. Harold used to hunt them. He carried two or three shot rabbits together, each by a hind leg. He came up the walk to their house carrying them, his gun in his other hand, and the free legs of the dead rabbits turning one way and then another around his wrist. It had been years since Harold had gone after rabbits.

The rabbit was still, but when Tyzack sat forward in his chair it stirred. He leaned down and reached his arm out to it, rubbing his fingers together as if trying to tempt a squirrel in a city park. The rabbit rose and crept away a little, then started and leaped. It landed halfway to the trees beyond the woodshed, where it stopped short, rising for another bound but arrested, backward looking, aware in that instant of Anne and Tyzack where they sat. Before the rabbit leaped again Anne could just make out, for the last time, its sidelong, wide eye.

★ ★ ★

Anne and Tyzack sat at the kitchen table eating lunch of crackers, soup, and beer. They talked about Harold.

"He is in Rutland?" Tyzack asked.

"He went with the truck," Anne said.

"Why did he have to take it there?" Tyzack asked. "What is wrong with it?"

"Nothing, but the radio stopped working, and they couldn't fix it right away except in Rutland. He'd rather have the radio work than the brakes," Anne said. "At his age."

"Yes," Tyzack laughed. "I don't suppose you could get him to come in and have a drink, later. When he comes for you . . . if Hugh is here by then," Tyzack said.

"No, probably not, if Hugh is here. He'll see Hugh's car in the driveway and wait out there."

"Should we hide his car?"

Anne laughed.

"They don't know each other," Tyzack said. "That's why they can't get on."

"Don't know each other?" Anne said. "I guess they do know each other. They have known each other all their lives. Yes, Harold was born October seventeenth and Hugh on Thanksgiving Day the same year. They're the same age. They're different types."

"Hugh wouldn't drive two hours to have his radio fixed," Tyzack said.

"He'd drive two hours to have it taken right out of the car," Anne said. "Hugh had rather radios had never been invented."

Anne took the soup bowls to the sink and cleared the other lunch things. She washed the bowls. Tyzack sat at the table and finished his beer. The afternoon was ahead.

He sat at his window. He read. Anne was busy elsewhere about the house or outdoors. Tyzack left the kitchen table and rolled into the sitting room.

At the window he saw one of the Wright sons go by in the road on a motorcycle. Tyzack watched him pass. The racket of the machine did not distress him. The young men in those parts didn't have much fun, Tyzack thought. What fun they had usually came from one or another piece of machinery. Still, young men everywhere will do what they like. Thirty years ago in

Berlin Tyzack had heard a commotion in the courtyard below his quarters and, looking out, watched half a dozen students in evening dress beat a goat to death with empty champagne bottles. It was at the same time, when Tyzack went out in the mornings, that he sometimes found the streets full of broken glass from the windows of the Jewish shops. These spirits in the best young men, and the glass on the sidewalks, in time led Tyzack to (the way Hugh put it) reflect, as a quarter-Jew, on the advantages of Anglo-American civilization, in which—again, according to Hugh—a reasonably sober white man had nothing to fear from any policeman unless his driver's license had expired.

★ ★ ★

In the kitchen Anne cleaned the sink. The kitchen windows looked west, and the kitchen itself was dark until mid-afternoon, though the backyard of the house was now filled with sunlight. Beyond the yard the hill rose in a long reach to its heights, which declined toward the south in a green curve nearly at the windows' top as you stood at the kitchen sink. The hillside was clear of trees except at the fence-lines. These made a great letter H upon the hill, the crossbar lying halfway between the house and the top of the hill. Anne could see cows at the hilltop. They were her brother's. As she watched, a few of them moved down from the hillside between the long fences. At that distance the black and white cows looked completely white, like lambs.

Anne got a ball of string and went out the back door of the kitchen. From the woodshed she took a bundle of stakes for tying up the flowers beside the house. If her brother was coming that evening, she would see to it that the flower bed had been cared for. Hugh owned the house, which he rented to Tyzack.

Anne ran a stake into the earth near the roots of the fallen flowers, then picked up several of the stalks and tied them. The flower bed was under the windows of Tyzack's bedroom and the other room at that side of the house. Working there, Anne was at the foundation of the house. The house was old, wood-framed. It sat on long stone blocks that lay at the level of the ground, on top of the cellar wall. The house was heavy on its foundations, carefully made and planned. Still, Anne thought, it had not been a rich man's house. The people who had built it, and those who had lived there until recently, would be accounted poor people today. Ordinary people couldn't any longer afford to live in such a house. Today, fortunate people lived in what had been ordinary people's houses, and ordinary people lived somewhere else. Anne and Harold weren't poor, but they lived near the highway in a small place they barely owned. Harold said a poor man couldn't even afford to get into debt any more.

Anne worked to prop up the fallen flowers. Tyzack always wanted her brother and Harold to get along. They never would. Nothing was at fault there. It wasn't necessary that the brothers-in-law get along. Still, Tyzack talked to her about it. He professed to be mystified that Harold was shy of Hugh, and Hugh so casual about Harold. Tyzack pretended to think that two men of the same age and antecedents, living in the same little American town, must be allies. It might have been a measure of his distance from them all, but in fact he knew better than he said.

Anne believed that the enduring things were

ordered. She would have asked Tyzack how it happened that his daughter didn't know where he was. She didn't ask because, though she knew no specific reasons and none of the history of Tyzack and his daughter, she knew their estrangement from living in it herself, from participating in a life that was ordered by it. If Tyzack's daughter had been a part of his life there would have been no need for Hugh to look out for him, no need for Anne to work for him. He wouldn't even be here. Why didn't Tyzack know his daughter? Why didn't Hugh and Harold get on? Why had Anne and Harold never had children? For these things to have been otherwise, time itself, and the weight of circumstances going back who knows how far, would have had to be ordered differently. They were ordered as they were. Things had to be settled some one way.

Inside, at his window, Tyzack read *The Eighteenth Brumaire of Louis Bonaparte.* He had come to believe that the only major authors who finally succeeded in making abstractions seem exciting or momentous were Marx and Plato. He was old, he said sometimes, and he wanted a bit of fun out of thought— the illusion that it was getting somewhere.

Tyzack had conversations about Marx with Hugh. On one of his visits Anne's brother had found Tyzack reading Marx, and they had talked about him. Tyzack could see it pleased Hugh to be discussing Marx in the sitting room of a farmhouse in New England.

Hugh had said that Marx never understood the country, life in the country, or country people. It was a flaw in Marx's thought, Hugh said. He asked Tyzack if he were a Communist.

"Socialist or Social Democrat," Tyzack said.

"They're just soft-hearted Communists, aren't they?" Hugh asked.

"The ones I knew weren't very soft-hearted," Tyzack said.

"They're wised-up Communists," Hugh said.

"Well," Tyzack said, "whatever they are, you're not one."

"I don't think so," Hugh said, laughing.

Beyond Tyzack's window the light was failing. The shadows of the trees ran downhill. At Wright's place a light went on. In late summer, when the sun gets down, the light does not linger. It goes away before your eyes, like water running out a drain. Tyzack returned to his book. The page was dark. He did not turn on the light.

★ ★ ★

There came the noise of a car rolling up the gravel drive, stopping. Tyzack had been asleep in his chair. He opened his eyes, looked out. The east held the last daylight, blue above purple clouds, but all about the house, in the road and in the meadow, was night. A car stood in the drive. While Tyzack watched, the car's lights went out, and Hugh opened the door and stood. Anne waited before the house. She called something to Hugh that Tyzack didn't hear.

"Sure," Hugh said. He shut the car door and approached the house.

Anne and Hugh entered the house, came into the sitting room to Tyzack.

"Well, Bruno," Hugh said.

"Well, well," said Tyzack. They shook hands.

"You're sitting in here in the dark," Hugh said.

"I was asleep," Tyzack said.

"Come in the kitchen," Anne said. "It's cold."

They followed her. Tyzack and Hugh sat at the kitchen table. Anne asked Hugh if he would stay for supper, and Hugh said he'd like to. Tyzack asked him if he wanted a drink, and he said he would. Anne put a stew pot on the stove. Hugh got up from the table and took a bottle of whiskey and glasses out of the kitchen cupboard. Anne got ice. Hugh put the bottle and glasses down before Tyzack and sat again. Tyzack poured out whiskey into three glasses. He handed Anne hers. She took it to the sink and filled the glass with water.

"Sit down, Mrs. Tavistock," Tyzack said.

"I'll stand over here so I can see Harold when he comes," Anne said. She stood by the side window.

"Harold," Hugh said. "How's Harold?"

"He's pretty well," Anne said.

"Oh, wait a minute," Hugh said. He went to the door and picked up a parcel he had set down there. "I brought you a couple of books," he said, and put the parcel on the table in front of Tyzack. Then he returned to his chair and picked up his glass.

"Well," said Hugh, and drank.

Anne said, "Cheers," and Tyzack nodded his head at Hugh and drank, then turned to Hugh's package.

"A couple of books?" he said. "Mrs. Tavistock said '*a* book.'"

"Well, there are two or three in there," Hugh said.

Tyzack was taking books out of the package. There were two paperbacks in French by Simenon, and a third by an author he didn't know. There was a larger volume, bound in boards, *Classiques Français du Moyen Age*. "These are fine," Tyzack said. "It's very good of you." He opened *Classiques Français* and began turning the pages. Anne went over and turned on another light for him, then returned to the window.

Tyzack paged through his new book; Anne waited by the window, sometimes looking out at the drive for Harold. Hugh drank his whiskey and looked here and there around the room and up at the corners of the ceiling, like the man who owns the house.

Tyzack spread the book on the table and held it open with his finger. He took a drink and read aloud.

> *Dictes moy ou, n'en quel pays,*
> *Est Flora la belle Rommaine,*
> *Archipiades ne Thais*
> *Qui fut sa cousine germaine,*
> *Echo parlant quant bruyt on maine*
> *Dessus riviere ou sus estan*
> *Qui beaulte ot trop plus qu'humaine?*
> *Mais ou sont les neiges d'antan?*

Anne glanced out the window. Their truck stood in the driveway behind Hugh's car. She could see Harold behind the wheel, looking out, not toward the house, but ahead. Anne went to the door, got her coat from its hook. "Here he is," she said.

"Get him in here," Hugh said. "He needs a drink."

Anne put on her coat. "No, I'd better go along," she said.

"Harold has come from Rutland this afternoon," Tyzack said to Hugh. "He will want to be on his way home. Thank you, Mrs. Tavistock," he said. "Have a nice evening."

"I'll see you tomorrow," Anne said. To her brother she said, "You'll be around for a while, will you?"

"Sure. I'll stop by tomorrow or the next day. Tell Harold I'll see him."

"Goodnight," Anne said. She went out. She closed the door after herself. The lights on their truck went on, the engine started. From outside the door Anne heard Hugh say, "Did he really go to Rutland because his radio was broken?" Anne got into the truck beside Harold.

"Hi, there," Harold said. His big face was on her for a moment, then turned to watch out the rear window as he let the truck roll back down the drive. "Hugh got in all right?" he said.

"About five or five-thirty," Anne said. "It was just dark."

Anne and Harold were in the road. Harold put the truck in gear, and they started down the hill. Anne looked at Tyzack's house where there was light in the window of the kitchen.

"They'll be at it to all hours, I expect," Harold said.

Hugh and Tyzack would sit in the kitchen with the light. They'd have another drink. They'd eat, talk, until Hugh had mercy on Tyzack and left him, sometime after midnight. What they talked about, thought about, and remembered together could never change. It was the two of them, Hugh and Tyzack, and the four of them, Hugh, Tyzack, Anne, and Harold; others, too, without number, populations living and dead, ordered individuals, minds, and works—Wrights; Hilde; Marx; talkative women who were Anne's neighbors; Stalin;

four years of shrill English schoolboys and their masters; spirited German youths of the junker class, all no doubt killed in the war; Louis Napoleon; boys in the village of Ambrose who cut firewood and brought it to the houses of working women and the old men who were in their care.

11

The BRIDE
of AMBROSE

The Mexican assistant for Inter-American affairs, whose name was Mendez Vargas, rose from his place at the table and passing behind my wife's seat, drew her chair out for her. Certainly he had perfect manners.

"Outdoors," he said. "Outdoors it will be pleasant."

Mendez Vargas gave my wife his arm and led her from the table, through French doors, and out onto a broad terrace. The rest of us were to follow them. We were four. Neville Mowbray, the film actor, whom we called "Stash," escorted young Mme. Mendez Vargas, and I wound up with Antoinette Blakemore, a childhood pal of my wife's whose current husband Mowbray was. Antoinette took my arm, and we followed Mowbray and Mme. Mendez Vargas onto the terrace.

"Fancy Stash and the enchilada," Antoinette said.

"The enchilada?" I said.

"Sure, the enchilada. The jalapeña."

173

"Now I get you," I said to Antoinette. "You're talking dirty."

"The tropics affect me," she said. "Is this the tropics?"

"Pretty near," I said.

"You don't change," Antoinette said. "Oh, just look at him."

Mendez Vargas and the two women had taken chairs on the terrace, but Neville Mowbray—Stash—had seated himself on the stone parapet. He had lit a cigarette, and now he swept it from his mouth with a large motion of his arm and lifted his chin. Displaying his ruined profile, he gazed off the terrace to where the land went down to the sea and the shore made a headland behind which were visible, blooming against night clouds, the lights of Mazatlán.

"Isn't he a beauty?" Antoinette said, as we sat down. "And he doesn't know it himself."

"Don't be ridiculous," I said. "Of course he knows it. He's vain as a peacock."

"You're wrong," Antoinette said. "You're always wrong."

"What are you saying?" Neville Mowbray asked us.

"We were saying what a beautiful specimen you are," Antoinette called out.

"I thank you," Mowbray said from his place on the parapet.

"My grandfather," Mendez Vargas was telling my wife, "made the property. It is jungle all along here, you see, all along the coast. He had a hundred men to clear land. He had to clear the jungle. He built his road. He cleared to the shore. He built the houses. Everything was jungle.

"Today," he said, "we have to keep clearing. Each year we chop and we—what?—we *mow.* Otherwise the jungle immediately grows back."

"It reminds me of Vermont," said my wife.

From the parapet Neville Mowbray spoke up. "Vermont?" he said. "Who knows Vermont?"

He was vain, Stash was, whatever Antoinette Blakemore believed. Nobody blamed him. The chin he tilted for us to admire had been a perfect chin twenty years ago: square, smooth, firm. It was still a fine chin, though worn down some. Stash himself was worn.

He was out of work. A public that had, at last, changed, and thirty hard years of drink and unwise living had about ended his employment as second lead in the trumped-up California epics that had been his occupation. Stash had been Jupiter, Pompey, Moses, Arthur, Henry VIII, Louis XIV, George III, Admiral Nelson, even Sitting Bull, even Kubla Khan—speaking the words of all of them indifferently in the accents of the British aristocracy, accents which, with the name and identity of Neville Mowbray, he had carefully acquired long ago to outfit his own magnificent good looks. For Neville Mowbray, the British actor, called "Stash" by his friends, had been born Stanislodz Lielujpovics in Riga to a Lettish father and a Polish mother. Stash learned his English on a dirty freighter, and later living in Halifax, Nova Scotia. England was one of the few countries in Europe where he had never been.

"Who knows Vermont?" Stash asked us.

"I come from there," I said.

"I know Vermont," Stash said. "Years ago I was there. Oh, thirty years. I was in New York, you know. My God, we drove for hours. I thought—I was not long in this country then, you know, and I thought we must be in California pretty soon. It was Vermont. Sure, I remember it. Totally remote. The girl I went there with was from there, too. Vermont, sure. We drove all one night, out of one of those little villages and into the next one." He looked down at me. "Which was yours?" he asked.

"Town of Ambrose," I said. "Down near Massachusetts."

"It's not near Massachusetts," my wife said. "It's nowhere near."

"Ambrose," said Stash. "Ambrose. Ambrose, Vermont. Sure. It's the same place, I think. Sure. Ambrose. I remember it. You come around a curve and the village is right there and the church, there, and a mountain up behind it? Am I right? Sure. The girl I drove with was from there, too. Maybe you knew her, too."

"I did," I said.

"You did?" my wife said. "How do you know?"

"Brenda Yarbrough," I said.

"That's her!" Stash said. "Brenda. Do you know where she is now?"

"No," I said.

"Cold," Stash said. "Totally cold. We were there in her house for the night—her sister's house, it was—and I never was so cold. And I came from a cold country, don't forget. That house. That village. No offense, you know, but that is one God-forsaken place."

"It's pretty in the fall," I said.

"Tell us about it, why don't you?" said Antoinette

Blakemore, and my wife said, "Yes, tell us. Tell us about the girl."

So Stash told us how he had come down to New York in 1950 as an ice-water wetback, down from Canada just at Christmas time. He told us about the next year, 1951, the year he knew Brenda, the year he got his agent, the year they decided that since he was in America he might as well go west and become a rich movie star like most other Americans.

At first, though, there weren't any Americans to be seen. Stash had crossed the border in the middle of the pine woods in Maine, found the highway, got a ride with a French Canadian who was on his way to Lowell, Massachusetts, where he fed Stash and passed him on to another French Canadian who was driving to New York.

In New York he had a small and dirty room uptown. His neighbors and the people on the streets and in the stores were Spanish or Irish, or they were Jews, or they were the same kind of homeless north European that Stash was.

He found a job as a messenger downtown. They gave him a gray uniform, a clipboard, a roll of nickels, and messages to carry in big yellow envelopes. He rushed around New York. The other messengers were Irish kids, or Italians; the supervisor was a Lebanese. They were all good to Stash. They took trouble for him because he was good-looking and because he was new, just as the Frenchmen had who had driven him down from Maine. But Stash wondered where the Americans lived. Where were the cowboys, the gangsters, the millionaires, the movie stars? When was he going to meet one of them?

"Well," Stash said, "one of the kids, the messengers, was named Coogan. And this kid wanted to be an actor. Now at this time I didn't have any idea about that myself. I was just working, just staying out of trouble, going home at night. But this Coogan was an actor. I mean, I don't know if he ever worked, but he took acting classes and he had lots of actor friends. And he went to rowdy parties all the time with them. So one time he said, there's a party at this girl's place. Why don't you come? And I said, you know, sure, because I was totally bored, really. And this Coogan gave me the address. What time should I come? I asked him, and he said, oh, about two. And I said, well, how can I? We've got to work then. And he said, no, I mean two in the morning.

"Well, okay. I went down there the night he said, and I could hear the party half a block away. I went in and there must have been a couple of hundred people in this little, little apartment, and everybody is totally drunk and yelling and carrying on, and in the front room a lot of people don't have any clothes on, and in the kitchen they are smoking loco weed. You know the kind of party. Oh, and then there are people painting each other, you know, with brushes and paint, and there was one guy who was trying to walk on a lot of broken glass."

He looked for Coogan, but Coogan wasn't there. Stash decided to leave, but he couldn't get out of the apartment because of the jam of people. He found himself shoved into a corner of a dark hallway. There was a commotion at the other end of the passage. A Negro who must have been half a foot taller than Stash was trying to make his way through the crush. In his arms he carried an unconscious woman.

"Excuse us, excuse us," the Negro said. "Come on, folks, gangway a little bit. Lady needs some air. Thank you, sir. Excuse us." He passed down the hall carrying the woman high in his arms. Stash could see a gold ring in the Negro's ear as he passed.

"Excuse me," somebody else was saying. Stash tried to press himself farther back into his corner. Who was coming now?

"Excuse me," the same voice said again. A girl was talking to Stash. "Mister, do you think you could get off? You're about standing on me." He turned to her.

"Oh, sure," Stash said. "Sorry."

"You did no harm," the girl said.

"I didn't know you were there," Stash said.

"I didn't suppose you did."

Stash asked the girl if she knew Coogan.

"What does he look like?" the girl said.

Stash found he didn't know what Coogan looked like.

The girl said, "I don't think I know him, at that."

"Well," Stash said, "do you know everybody here?"

"Do I look like it?"

"What?" Stash said.

"Do I look like I know them?" she said.

"I don't know," Stash said, "I don't know."

"I know some of them," the girl said then. "They are all crazy. A lot of them know the man I work for. Probably you know him, too. Are you a performer?"

Stash told her he wasn't and asked her who it was she worked for that everybody knew.

"Nastar Radash," the girl said.

"Who?" Stash said. He couldn't hear her for the racket of the party.

The girl stood on her toes and leaned toward his ear.

"Nastar Radash," she said.

At that moment the lights came on in the hallway, and Stash got a good look at her: her lips moving as she spoke close to him; her hair; her gray eyes that looked past him an instant when the light came on, then looked into his face, then at his mouth.

"I work for Nastar Radash," she said. She smiled.

It came to Stash that at last he had met, almost certainly, an American.

"So the lights are on," Stash said. Seated on the parapet before us, he reached above his head as if to turn on a light. "So the lights are on. And there are all these total drunks carrying on, and then it looked like somebody else was trying to get in, banging on the door. They came in, and it was about four or five cops, you know, and the noise went down a little. We could hear sirens: more cops coming. So they were raiding the party, which was out of control and should have got raided a couple of hours before, but I didn't like it because, you know. I was totally illegal in the U.S. I slipped over the border up there, and I didn't have any what do you call it. The paper. To stay? So I said, I've got to go, and the girl said, don't worry, they'll just take us to the precinct or whatever and pretty soon they'll let us go. Not me, I said, and I told her about no paper and everything. And she said, come with me."

The girl took Stash's hand and led him through the crowd to the back of the apartment and out the kitchen door. On the back stairs landing was another policeman.

"I can't let you out," he said. "Everybody is going downtown."

"My friend is ill," she said. "He's getting ready to be sick."

The landing was small. The three of them stood close together. The cops inside were big, but this cop was little. Stash stood over him. Stash moaned and clapped his hand to his mouth. He leaned toward the little cop.

"It's like I told you," the girl said.

"Christ, get him out of here," the cop said. He stood by, and Stash and the girl ran down the stairs. They went around behind the building next door and came out onto the street at a distance from the building where the party had been. Three police cars were standing in front, and people were coming out.

"This isn't good," the girl said. "What if they hold The Great Griswold?"

"Who is he? Your boyfriend?" Stash asked her.

"No, Griswold's a magician," the girl said. "You know—magic? He's got a kids' party tomorrow, and if they hold him he'll miss it and Nastar will get in trouble."

They started walking down the wet streets. The buildings were dark, and between the streetlights the streets were dark too. They were walking on the south side of the street, and the stone steps of the houses they passed went up on their right, one set of steps, then another, then another, all alike, all dark.

"That's some accent you have," the girl said. "Are you a German?"

"No, no," Stash said.

In the street they saw a man leading a big horse. The horse pulled a wagon that was piled up with metal: bedsprings, a stove, a car bumper, busted kitchen chairs, old water pipes, other metal junk.

"That's the kind of horse we use for plowing," the girl said. Her name was Brenda Yarbrough.

"Plowing?" Stash asked.

"Where I come from," the girl said. "Up the country."

★ ★ ★

They became friends, and nobody knew. Brenda guided Stash. She was Stash's map. In the brawl of tongues around him, in the scrabble of desperate greenhorns who could barely find their way, she was where she belonged and knew all the customs. Did Stash have a bad tooth? Brenda knew a dentist you didn't have to pay right away. Did Stash's friend Coogan quickly grasp the fact that Stash, however broke he was, would always have money for the wrong people? Brenda advised caution.

"Coogan," Stash told us. "Coogan needed a hundred dollars. He had a sister, a little kid, and she was blind. But there was an operation she could have that would make her see, Coogan said. The operation cost a hundred dollars, and Coogan didn't have it. And I said, you know, oh, gee, the poor little kid. Well, sure, I haven't got a hundred, but I can probably let you have seventy-five, anyway. And Coogan said, well, seventy-five would be better than nothing."

Brenda sighed when Stash told her about Coogan's blind sister. "Did you give him the money?" she asked.

"Not yet," Stash said. "I'll have to get it."

Brenda called Stash "Stan." She was the only one ever to give him that name.

"Stan," she said, "what if it's not true?"

"What?" Stash said.

"Look, Stan. This man wants a hundred dollars from you. It seems as though that is all you know for sure. What if the rest—about his blind sister—is something he saw in a movie?"

"You think he's lying about his sister?" Stash asked.

"I think that's real likely, yes," Brenda said.

"No," Stash said.

"Well," Brenda said. "That's fine, then. It's a good story, all right. You believe him, do you?"

"Well, sure I do," said Stash. "Well, I don't know."

"Stan," Brenda said. "Look. You've got to not be dumb. There are people who will rob you if you're dumb. I don't mean just thieves, but people you know, your friends, people who'd probably help you if you needed them. Some of them will rob you, anyway, if they can. It doesn't mean anything. They like you, but they don't care. It's like if you had a dog. The dog's your friend, he loves you, even. But he'll take your dinner if you leave it on the floor."

On the parapet where he sat, Stash puffed his

cigarette. He smiled. "So then I went back to Coogan, and I told him I wasn't going to give him the money, and I told him I thought his story about his blind sister was, you know, a bunch of crap.

"And I thought Coogan might come after me when I said that about his sister, because what if it was true? But all he said was, well, let's go get a beer."

In New York it's hot in the summer—everybody knows that—and always, the poorer you are the hotter it is. Neither Brenda nor Stash had any money, so they couldn't do much. They went to the movies to get cool. They went to the park. They hadn't any plans. They sat in Brenda's apartment with an electric fan pointed at them. Every window in the building would be open, and you could hear talking, shouting, radios, pots and pans, and from the street car horns, sirens, more shouting. Brenda talked about the country.

"At home," she said, "you can go up the hill a little and sit down in the grass, and there's no sound at all. It's dark, and it's so still because when it's hot I guess the frogs and peepers and them are quiet. You see how quiet it is, and pretty soon you don't feel the heat as much."

"So what do you do then?" Stash asked her.

"Well, you just sit out there, and then you get up and go back inside."

"I don't know," Stash said. "So what, you know?"

"Well," Brenda said. "It's nice. There's not a lot of smells and noise. The air is good. It's beautiful."

Brenda was quiet for a moment. "The thing is, Stan," she said, "there's nothing to do. It's nice, but it's always the same. The thing of it is, it's nice, but you can live your whole life there."

Brenda was sitting on the bed. She looked at Stash.

"They don't care," she said. "Robbie. Robbie doesn't care. He'd just as soon be there. Robbie will never leave. But I don't know."

"Is he your boyfriend?" Stash asked.

From the parapet Stash shot the end of the cigarette he had been smoking out into the dark. We all watched it silently. It fell like a tiny rocket into the garden.

"I didn't make a big play for Brenda, or anything," Stash went on after a moment. "I thought about it. She was not bad-looking at all, and so at first I thought she had lots of boyfriends, but then I found out she didn't, you know, go out much. So then I figured, she and her boss, Nastar Radash, that she was something for the office for Nastar. But I couldn't believe it. The pope would cheat on his wife before Nastar. So I didn't know. Maybe she had a boyfriend at home where she came from, in the country. If that was it, though, why was she living in New York? I didn't get it. But then at that time there were a lot of things I didn't get about—not just Brenda, you know—but about America.

"See, for one thing, I thought she was rich. She would tell me about her family's place, the land, the house, the barns, the cows, horses, cars. And so I thought, for sure, a rich farmer, you know, because where I came from only the rich had a place like that. But I found out her father had nothing—well, not nothing; he had a place just like she said, the farm—but he was totally not rich. You could have all that stuff and still not be rich."

"You could, then," I said.

"Sure," Stash said. "Then."

"Who was Nastar Radash?" my wife said.

★ ★ ★

Nastar Radash had his office in a crummy building west of Broadway. You went to the seventh floor in an elevator that smelled funny. You got out on a long gloomy hall of silent offices that looked as though they belonged to mail-order private investigators. In fact it was a good building, but it didn't have a lot of put-up. What there was was in the offices of Radash Talent Associates, where in the reception room Nastar had years ago hung—in a band running around the top of the four walls—fancy photographs of actors, singers, other performers, all famous and none represented by him, then or ever. You were to infer that these figures—Tyrone Power, W. C. Fields, Joan Fontaine, and so on—were Nastar's clients, or at least his friends. They weren't. Nastar's clients were ventriloquists, prestidigitators, and poor comics, and his friends were unknown. He was an honest man who worked hard to get by, and he was a sad man, made so no doubt by the misfortunes of his country, one of the small states of eastern Europe whose people had been scattered, thrashed, starved, and forgotten for a hundred years. For such of them as had reached the United States Nastar Radash was adviser, interpreter, matchmaker, banker, and postman. He was also the editor and publisher of *Liberatyi Balkannyi,* circulation one thousand, a small newspaper for the émigré community.

Brenda wanted Stash to talk to Nastar, but Stash wasn't sure. He didn't see what Nastar could do for him.

Stash was afraid to claim his destiny. When Brenda told him he ought to quit being a messenger and let Nastar try to get him a walk-on in a play or a job modeling men's clothes, he said, "Why should I? It's a good job."

"Stan, come on," Brenda said.

"What's wrong with being a messenger? What are you doing that's so much better?"

"I'm here, aren't I?" Brenda said. "That's not bad."

"I'm here, too," said Stash. "That's not bad, either. I came a longer way to get here than you did."

"You're not happy," Brenda said.

"Who says so? Sure I am. And anyway, how come you can just be here and I've got to do something?"

What did Brenda do, anyway? She was Nastar Radash's assistant, but Radash Talent Associates was the two of them, no one else. What was the story on Brenda and Nastar Radash? Stash went to see for himself.

The obscure street entrance to Nastar's building, the unprepossessing lobby, the dirty elevator, the lugubrious corridor: these Stash took in. At the door of Radash Talent Associates, he entered and walked in on Brenda and Nastar Radash. They were sorting through piles of newspapers. *Liberatyi Balkannyi* had been printed that morning, and the new copies had to be separated and mailed. Stash stood in the open office door before Brenda and Nastar.

"Mr. Radash," Brenda said. "This is my friend, Stanislodz Lielujpovics."

"Lielujpovics? What is he?" Nastar said to Brenda, "some kind of Russian?"

Before us on the terrace Stash held out his hand, low, to indicate a short person, then hunched his shoulders.

"Nastar Radash," he said, "was a little guy. He was the guy with the most hair I ever saw. Not long hair, but lots of hair, totally black hair, growing out of his eyebrows, out of his ears, out of his nose. My God, naked he must have looked like a little grizzly bear.

"He wouldn't talk to me at all. He'd talk to Brenda about me and never talk right to me. And that got met, you know? I thought he did it to put me down, and I thought, *That hairy ape, and her.* But really he did it because he's totally shy, he's too shy to talk to you at first. That was all it was.

"But anyway, Nastar said, what does he do? And Brenda said, he's an actor. And I said, no. But Nastar paid no attention. Well, he looks like an actor, he said, and I shut up then."

Nastar Radash got up from the desk where he sat and walked around the office looking at Stash from different parts of the room. He turned off the ceiling light, turned it on. "Boy," he said. "You can't say he doesn't look right."

"He wants to get started," Brenda said. "And I thought George always needs somebody."

"He couldn't have any lines," Nastar said.

"No, but just to get him around a picture," Brenda said.

"I don't know," Nastar said. "You shouldn't be in a hurry. Sure, I could get him in with George. Maybe I could. But George isn't doing anything until next year, and anyway George is stupid. George will just see his crazy name and that he can hardly talk English, and George will give him a job as a favor to me and then he'll forget him. We got time. We ought to give him a little working on, then maybe George will see him and really help him, or maybe then we can do better than George."

"How long?" Brenda asked.

"I don't know," Nastar said. "Six months? Eight months? Is he eating? Has he got time? I said we had time, but maybe we don't. Maybe he doesn't have time."

"I got time," Stash said.

"Okay," Nastar said. "We'll need Pennyroyal for him, and he ought to get started. Can he pay her?"

"I can pay her," Stash said. "Who is she?"

"She's a speech coach," Brenda said. "For working on your accent."

"Is she an acting teacher?" Stash asked. He was thinking of his friend Coogan, who took acting lessons. Nastar Radash spoke to him for the first time.

"She's no acting teacher," he said. "You don't need that junk. Acting is just walking around and talking. Pennyroyal helps with the talking, and the rest you can do or you can't."

"Okay," Stash said.

Jessica Pennyroyal was not a New Yorker. She did not correct people who believed that she was the daughter of Sir William Pennyroyal, Privy Councillor, and an English gentlewoman currently living in New York in reduced circumstances; neither did she deny that she had been born in Erie, Pennsylvania, to a family of alcoholic vaudevillians. She might have been forty, she might have been seventy: gray-haired, high-necked, having a dutiful democratic charm but with it a blue eye like a cold northern ocean—a gracious lady in the British manner, but one who had to make the rent. Her work she called helping people learn to speak English, and she was one of the last people in the city, even then, who knew exactly how to do their job.

Miss Pennyroyal lived alone in three rooms of a house on Eleventh Street that had once been owned by Alexander Hamilton. Her rooms were on the ground floor, going from the street front of the house to a little garden in back. She met with her speech pupils in the long front room. Nastar Radash, Brenda, and Stash called on her there.

Introduced to Stash, Jessica Pennyroyal sat him down beside her chair, patted his arm to put him at his ease, asked him where he lived, what he did, how long he had been in New York. She wanted to hear him talk. She did not take Stash for a German. She did not take him for a Russian.

"You poor man," she said. "I think you must have come from a Captive Nation, haven't you? So sad."

Miss Pennyroyal was pleased with Stash. "You talk from here," she said later, laying her hand on her chest, "and not from here," touching her throat. "Do you know how important that is? Without it we would have so much work to do. As it is, we can simply have fun. You're to come every Monday, Wednesday, and Friday afternoon between five and six. Now, mind you, I must charge ten dollars a visit. You pay as you go. Will that do?"

"Sure," said Stash.

"Sure," said Nastar Radash.

"So," said Jessica Pennyroyal. She waited.

Stash was broke. Miss Pennyroyal looked from him to Nastar. Nastar got out his wallet and handed her a ten-dollar bill, which she slipped fastidiously under a napkin on the table beside her chair. From the same table she took a book, opened it to a marked page, and handed it to Stash.

"I like to start at the top and then work toward the bottom so as to end up back at the top," she said. "It's my method. Read that to me, Mr. Lielujpovics."

Stash began to read the passage. Midway through his reading, Miss Pennyroyal left her chair and crossed to the end of the room. When Stash paused, she said, "I can't hear you, Mr. Lielujpovics. You must read louder. Please start again."

Stash read again: "Now is the winter of our discontent/Made glorious summer by this sun of York. . . ."

When he finished, he was sweating, he was breathing hard. From the end of the room where she had been listening, Jessica Pennyroyal beamed at the three of them.

"You see?" she said. "Anyone can learn to speak English. Absolutely anyone."

Through the summer and fall, and into the winter, Stash and Jessica Pennyroyal worked. Miss Pennyroyal's methods were undoubtedly her own. Sometimes she made Stash sing, sometimes she made him hum. Sometimes he read to her from Shakespeare and *Paradise Lost,* sometimes he read nursery rhymes, jokes, and stories from the *Daily News.* Gradually Miss Pennyroyal led Stash on ways that left Shakespeare behind. She told him to listen to the news and advertising announcers on the radio. He had no radio. When she saw he couldn't afford to buy one, she gave him her own radio.

For some weeks Stash and Miss Pennyroyal worked on radio voices and read the *Daily News.*

" 'Guard slen,' " Stash read.

"No, Mr. Lielujpovics," said Miss Pennyroyal. "You're to say *slain* to rhyme with *pain*, not to rhyme with *hen.* Read it again, please."

" 'Guard slein. Three flee.' "

"*Slain,*" Miss Pennyroyal said.

Presently she began to bring him back up. He read Dickens to her. He read *Paradise Lost* again. Shakespeare.

Sometimes Nastar Radash and Brenda went with Stash to Jessica Pennyroyal's. One day before their session began Miss Pennyroyal handed Nastar a slip of paper on which she had written *Neville Mowbray.*

Miss Pennyroyal had found the name in *Burke's Peerage.*

"He's a baronet, or was, poor man," she said. "So sad. Killed on the Somme."

"Good luck to him," said Nastar Radash.

"Of course, Mr. Lielujpovics needn't be a baronet," Jessica Pennyroyal said. "That would hardly be appropriate."

"*Neville Mowbray,*" Brenda said.

Two weeks later Nastar Radash got Stash a part in a small production of a Shaw play. When the play closed, Nastar got him into a model agency. Stash traveled with a lot of other young men uptown to The Cloisters and posed wearing an expensive raincoat and looking earnestly at a wristwatch that was not his, while his picture was taken by a photographer. Stash quit his messenger job. Nastar found a part for him in another Shaw play.

"All they were was total talking," Stash said. "And that's what I knew how to do by that time." Jessica Pennyroyal had pronounced him nearly fit. Nastar

got him a part in a Broadway musical about Marco
Polo.

★ ★ ★

Today you can have a five-dollar drink for the road at a
clever little place in Manhattan at noon, climb in your
car, and be in Brattleboro, Vermont, in plenty of time to
have another five-dollar drink before dinner at another
little place only slightly less clever; but thirty-five years
ago, when Brenda and Stash drove up to that country,
the trip went on forever.

You went over the Triborough Bridge out of
New York, made the long, dry passage of the Bronx,
hacked a path through White Plains, and got on the
Merritt Parkway. You took the Merritt east, across Con-
necticut, to New Haven, where you found Route 5,
which came from beyond the edge of the known world.
There you turned north.

For hours, then, you followed Route 5 along the
river and the railroad, through farmland, villages, towns,
through Hartford, through Springfield, heading north.
The hills began in the distance, then they came close. At
Brattleboro or at Bellows Falls you left the highway and
went north by west on narrow roads into the hills: out of
one little village and into the next. There were woods,
or narrow meadows, then a house, then another, a concrete bridge over a small stream bed full of stones, then
two or three houses with porches, a store with a gas
pump, a post office with a flag, a patch of grass, a war
memorial, big trees, a church, a house, another house, a
barn, and then the woods again. Brenda drove until they
were out of the city. Then Stash drove.

They had Nastar Radash's car. He had given it to Brenda for the weekend. They were going to Ambrose, Vermont, Brenda's town, to see her nephew on his first birthday.

"This nephew, this baby, was called Billy or Johnny, or like that," Stash said. "Her sister's baby. I got the total story on all of them driving up there, but I don't remember all their names. Let's see. The sister was Brenda's older sister, and her husband was, you know, George or Paul. He was a what-do-you-call-it? He chopped down trees. A lumberjack."

"A logger," I told Stash.

"Did you know him, too?" my wife asked me.

"Whatever," Stash said. Sitting on the parapet he turned and looked out over the bay. Far out the lights of a large boat passed in the darkness, a high topmast light blinking on and off. Stash turned back to us.

"The sister," Stash said. "She was older than Brenda. A good deal older, I think. She and George, or Paul, had married right out of school, but they had never been able to have any kids. Until they had this Billy or Jackie, or whatever. And Brenda was telling me how tickled they were—George or Paul and her sister—because they've been married all this time and wanted kids, and no kids. And now suddenly—you get it. So he and what's her name are totally tickled.

"Anyway, we're driving along and she's filling me in on everybody and going through the stuff she's brought for the baby. She's got this furry bunny that you wind up, and it, you know, wiggles its ears or something. Brenda wound it up and it went. She asked me how I liked it, and I guess I said it was all right. To tell the truth, I was getting totally bored with all the driving.

You know how you sit there driving the car and you feel the wheels going around down there under your ass and you're not getting any closer? So Brenda asked me what was the matter and I guess I said, you know, nothing."

They got to Ambrose after midnight. They drove through the dark village, past the shadowed houses that showed no light except when the headlights of their car passed the windows, momentarily shining on the black glass. Brenda's sister's house was at the end of the village. There was a dirt driveway beside the house. Stash turned the car in there, stopped, shut off the lights and the engine. He started to get out of the car.

"Wait," Brenda said.

"What?" Stash said.

"Stay here," Brenda said. "We can't wake them up."

"What do you mean, wake them up?" Stash said. "They're waiting for us, aren't they?"

"No," said Brenda.

"Wait a minute," Stash said. "Don't they know we're coming?"

"No," said Brenda.

"Oh, come on," Stash said. "Why not?"

"I didn't tell them."

"Oh, come on," Stash said. "I'm not sitting out here all night."

A window went up in the dark house, and somebody inside said, "Who is that?" Brenda opened the door of the car and got out.

"It's Brenda," she said.

"Brenda?" said the voice in the house. It was a woman.

"We drove up," Brenda said. "I'm with a friend."

"I didn't suppose you were by yourself. Just a minute," the woman said. "It's Brenda," she said to somebody in the house. The window closed. Inside the house a light went on, and a door opened. A woman in a robe left the house and came to the car. Stash could see a man standing in the open doorway.

"Oh, Bren," said the woman. She and Brenda embraced.

"This is my friend Stan," Brenda said. Brenda's sister looked into the car at Stash. "Well, you'd better both come in," she said. The three of them went toward the lighted door, where the man waited for them.

"Hi, Bren," he said.

"Hi, Wendell," Brenda said. "This is Stan, Wendell."

Stash and Wendell shook hands.

"You drove clear up from the city?" Wendell asked Stash.

"Uh. That's right," Stash said.

"Gee," Wendell said. "How did you come—up Five?"

Stash looked at him, shook his head. "I don't know," he said.

Stash and Wendell and the two women stood in the kitchen. In another room a baby began to cry.

"He heard you," Brenda's sister said. "I'll go get him. Do you want to come?" she asked Brenda.

"I don't know," Brenda said.

"Come on, Bren," her sister said. Together they went to get the baby. Stash and Wendell were left alone in the kitchen.

"Might as well come in here," said Wendell. They went into another room where the lights were on. There was bumpy linoleum on the floor and a small rug nailed down in the middle of the room, a big table, several straight chairs, a soft chair, a baby's playpen, an iron stove for heat with its pipe going into the plaster wall.

"What time did you get off?" Wendell asked Stash.

"What?" Stash asked.

"What time did you leave New York?" Wendell asked.

"Uh. I guess about noon," Stash said.

"You made good time, then," said Wendell. "Yes, Route Five is good. Or you could have come over Nine. Might have been quicker. But Five is always good."

Brenda and her sister came back into the room. Brenda's sister held the baby. He was wrapped in blankets, resting on her shoulder. The baby was quiet. He might have been asleep. Brenda sat down at the table, and her sister handed her the baby.

"You hold him, Bren," she said. Brenda held the baby awkwardly, and he struggled on her lap.

"Just sit him up, Bren," Brenda's sister said.

"No, not now," said Brenda.

"All right," her sister said. She took the baby from Brenda's lap.

"It was funny, because the sister looked a lot like Brenda," Stash told us. "But she looked like her, like she could be her mother, not her sister. She was older than Brenda, but she couldn't have been as much older as she looked. She was one of those totally serious women that looked like they never had a good time. A totally no-fun woman. Brenda was sitting there with the kid on her lap like it was a bomb that was about to go off. And the sister was just kind of watching them. The whole weekend was like that.

"I went out to the car for cigarettes. Nobody came after me, so, you know, after a while, I got into the back and went to sleep."

When Stash woke, the sun was well up. All the windows of the car were fogged over. He rubbed a clear spot and looked out. The ground was covered with wet dead leaves. He could see, down the road, the white houses of the village with the simple morning sunlight on them.

Brenda's sister's house was quiet. Everyone was still asleep. Wendell wasn't there. He had left for work hours before.

Stash got out of the car and walked around behind the house. Back there were a clothes line and an old truck sitting on its axles, with weeds growing up around it. Beyond the truck, grass full of fallen leaves, then taller grass sloping down to a line of woods a hundred feet behind the house. A stone wall grown up with trees and brambles went toward the woods. Stash followed the wall to the woods. He found a brook running hard over brown stones. Stash stepped across it.

Now the land went gradually up. When Stash looked back he couldn't see the brook, he couldn't hear it. He might have been lost out in the middle of the woods, but he saw ahead of him the wall among the trees, and, beyond it, sunlight on open land.

Stash stood inside the woods at the edge of a large sunny meadow. The grass was short and brown, and the ground hard. Beyond the meadow the hills went off to the west. He had come to a corner of the meadow, and opposite him, across the open mowing, he saw a man walking along the edge of the woods. The man saw Stash and started toward him across the meadow, as though Stash's arrival had freed the man from whatever purpose kept him there.

The man came to Stash, and Stash saw he was some kind of hunter. He was tall and wore tan pants, a red shirt, and a tan canvas coat. Under his arm he carried a shotgun. The man said, "Been out since sunup and haven't seen a goddamned one." He gave Stash a careful look, not an unfriendly look: one that meant the man knew Stash didn't belong around here, but it wasn't his land they were on and so wasn't his business, though he'd remember having seen Stash there.

The hunter went on past Stash, mounted the stone wall, and stepped heavily down into the woods. He was not a young man. He went deeper into the woods, going back in the direction from which Stash had come. Some man from the town.

Stash heard Brenda calling him from the house and went back through the woods and across the brook. He expected to find Brenda talking with the hunter, but when he came back up toward the house she was alone in the yard. The hunter had gone off some other way.

"Where were you?" Brenda asked Stash.

"I don't know. I went for a walk."

"Where were you last night?"

"I slept in the car," Stash said.

"They had a room all set for you, Stan. What was the matter?" They went into the house.

"Well," Stash said, "I just conked out in the car."

"So we went in and sat in the kitchen, and everybody had a cup of coffee," Stash told us. "And that's it: there's nothing to do. I liked a little action then, you know? Even a broke immigrant can usually get up some kind of action. In New York, you know, you'd do—what?—you'd go to the movies or you'd go get something to eat, get on the street. But here there's nothing like that. Everybody sits around. I mean, it was very strange.

"I thought the sister was unhappy because I slept in the car. Or she might have been like that all the time. Anyway, she was in the house making a cake, for the baby's birthday. And she was beating up the cake in this bowl she had. So I thought I'd be extra nice to her, Brenda's sister, you know. It so happens when I was a kid, I worked for a baker once. And I did all that mixing and beating, all day. That is hard work, don't kid yourself. So I told the sister something like, you know, gee, I know how hard that is, that beating, because I used to work for a baker. And she said, well, we're going to get an electric beater. So that was the end of that conversation.

"Then I tried being nice to the baby. The baby was on Brenda's lap there in the kitchen, so I got down on the floor and I, you know, made faces at him and made funny noises. And he didn't mind, but he just sat there in her lap and looked at me. Even the little babies there didn't have anything to do and just looked at you, you know?"

Stash has been ill at ease no more than two or three times in his life, I expect. That morning in the kitchen in Ambrose may have been the first time ever.

He didn't know how to handle it. The truth is, those self-possessed infants up in Vermont have brought down far tougher cases than Stash.

"Finally they decided to go for a drive," Stash said. "Look at the trees, you know? But I was ready. Was I ready? I jumped up, like *zing,* and I said, 'Sure, sure, come on, let's go.' I had to get out of there."

Stash drove. Brenda's sister sat beside him in front, and Brenda and the baby sat in back. They drove out of the village and along the river beside brown stubble fields. They turned right and went up into the hills. The road went through woods, but the houses they passed sat before cleared fields or pastures that reached to the tops of the hills behind them. There were cows in several of the pastures and, at one place, sheep. In the woods there was water everywhere: in brooks that ran in steep ravines, in springs and seeps that ran beneath the road through culverts, in ponds and swamps to either side.

They went around a corner, and Brenda's sister said, "There it is, Bren."

"There it is," said Brenda from the back seat.

Through the trees that grew along the road Stash could see, set up on the bank, a big white house with low buildings built off the end connecting to a tall barn with a stone foundation. In front of the barn some men were cutting cordwood on a buzz saw that was hooked up to a tractor. You could hear the blade when the men put a stick to it.

"That's our house," Brenda said.

Stash let the car slow down, but Brenda's sister said, "Don't stop," and they drove on past. From the back seat, where she watched the men in the yard through the car's rear window, Brenda asked, "Is that Robbie?" and her sister said, "Must be."

"Is he your boyfriend?" Stash asked Brenda. The road went into the woods again.

"We got back to the house, and the sister's husband was home from work. And anyway, Brenda said she was going to lie down until supper. I don't know, something was the matter. So I went with her to the room she had, and I said, you know, what's the matter? And she said, nothing—I shouldn't have come. And I said, well, let's go. And she said, we'll go tomorrow. Why don't we go tonight, I said. We could be back tomorrow morning. And Brenda said, you know, if you want to go, go, but I'm staying 'til tomorrow. And so I said okay. How was she going to get back without me?"

★ ★ ★

Late that night Stash woke up.

He had been sleeping in a little spare room upstairs. The night was full of moonlight that poured in his window. Stash got up from the mattress and went to the window. Above the village, the moon burned, so bright that no stars were visible and objects cast gray shadows. In the road in front of the house Brenda stood in her nightdress, white like the houses, the trees, the ground the moon shone on. She was in the middle of the roadway, turning slowly around and around in the same spot. She was barefoot, and her hair hung down her back. Stash looked down on her from his window in the house. Brenda stopped turning and got down on her knees in the road. Then she lay down full length on her stomach, pressing her cheek to the dirt.

A door shut under his window, and Stash saw

Brenda's sister leave the house and walk down to Brenda. Brenda's sister was also in her nightdress, but her hair was done in a long braid behind, and she was wearing slippers. She stood over Brenda and seemed to talk to her. Then she knelt beside Brenda. Brenda raised her face from the road, and together the two women looked off toward the village. Brenda got to her feet, and she and her sister walked slowly back to the house. Her sister's arm was around Brenda's waist, holding her. They went in. The door shut. The moonlight lay on the pale road where Brenda had been.

"I thought, well, I won't say anything about this," Stash remembered, "but I was going to be just as glad to get out of there and back to New York. I tried to go back to sleep, but it was cold in that room. I couldn't get warm. Totally cold. So I finally sneaked downstairs and out to the car, and I turned the engine on and the heater. I spent the rest of that night in the car, too. But I slept."

Sunday morning Wendell helped Stash carry their things to the car. The women were in the house. At the car Wendell stopped Stash for a minute.

"How has she been?" he asked, and Stash said, "Uh. Pretty good. Well, I mean, you know."

Wendell nodded. "It's not easy on her," he said. "Everybody around here . . . well, I don't know if it's the right thing."

"Sure," Stash said.

"Well, you'll look out for her," Wendell said, and Stash thought, *Wait a minute.*

Brenda came out of the house with her sister and the baby, who slept. The four of them stood around the car. Brenda's sister held the baby. Brenda gave the baby a kiss that wouldn't wake him, embraced her sister, embraced Wendell. Stash was already behind the wheel. He started the engine. Wendell came around to him.

"Are you going back down Five?" he said.

"What?" Stash said.

"You could go over Nine and then down. You go through Bennington. Might be quicker."

"Oh, yeah. Yeah." Stash pumped the engine. Brenda got in the car. Wendell and Brenda's sister stepped back. They waved.

Stash felt like someone who is walking down the street when a bad accident takes place a block ahead. He was glad he didn't know exactly what had happened. He could turn the corner and not pass that way. Driving back down out of the hills toward the highways, he felt free. Brenda had cheered up, too, but she was tired. Stash was waiting to see what she would say to him on their long drive back to New York.

"Well, Stan, what do you say?" Brenda asked him. "Did you like being a Vermonter?"

"Too cold," Stash said. "I was never so cold as last night. You weren't cold last night?"

"I was fine," said Brenda.

On the terrace with us, Stash coughed and took from his pocket an enormous silk handkerchief with which he touched his lips.

"See?" he said. "I wanted to hear what she'd say. You know, if she'd say, like, boy, I had this crazy dream, and when I woke up, where do you think I was? If she'd say something about going out into the road. But all she said was, I was fine.

"She went to sleep someplace after we were down out of Vermont. And I just drove along. I was just as glad she was asleep. I stopped and got gas. She didn't wake up, and I just went on and didn't stop for lunch or anything. So we made pretty good time. And then late that afternoon we're coming down into the Bronx there, I'll never forget this," Stash said.

"See, we'd decided she'd drive in the city and I'd drive out in the country where there was no traffic because in case we had an accident, with me still not having any driver's license or visa or whatever—though Nastar was supposed to be fixing that. But when we got near New York she was sleeping, and so I kept on driving. And I'm really worried about it, you know? I'm holding on to the steering wheel, and I'm looking around and around and trying to drive real carefully. And going along. And then this cop car swings out and comes up right behind us. And he just hangs back there, following me along. That's right, a cop. And I am really sweating, and thinking of all the things that could happen. We'll get pulled over, you know, and the cop will ask for my license, and I'll get kicked out of the country, so forth. And we're driving along coming into New York in the Bronx somewhere, and I'm looking in the mirror all the time, and there's the cop car still behind me. Following. And then he pulls out and he passes. As he goes by, the cop waves to me. A real nice, polite wave, this nice-looking young cop in his cop car. He pulls away, and that's all: we're okay. Up ahead you can just see the towers of the bridge that we'll go over to get back to New York. And I thought then, you know: well, that cop might have stopped me, but he didn't. And now it's going to be okay."

★ ★ ★

At last Stash was headed west. "Several things are breaking on the coast about now," Nastar Radash told him.

"There ought to be something for you. I'm in touch. I'll talk to you." But a couple of weeks passed. Stash heard nothing from Nastar. It was Jessica Pennyroyal who gave him the word.

"Mr. Lielujpovics, you're to call on Mr. Radash tomorrow," Miss Pennyroyal told Stash when he arrived for his lesson one evening.

"I'll call him now," Stash said.

"Tomorrow will be time enough," Miss Pennyroyal said. "Mr. Lielujpovics, I expect Mr. Radash has found an opportunity for you out of town. If that is the case then our work together is at an end, which is cause for regret to me. But in any event," Miss Pennyroyal went on, "I can't have taken your money for much longer, you know. What you and I can do we have finished. You can speak English. You can even speak English verse a little—much good it will do you.

"You will never be an actor, Mr. Lielujpovics," she said. "But if you rely on Mr. Radash, and others of his type, you ought to be able to make a living, even to do well. You are a nice young man, and you're nice looking, to say the least. You want to guard against being stupid."

"I don't understand," Stash told her.

"Well, I can't say more," Miss Pennyroyal said. "Good luck, Mr. Lielujpovics."

The next day Nastar took Stash over to Broadway and bought him an orange juice in a place Nastar said performers went to. Nastar gave Stash the deal. In a month production would start in Los Angeles on a lousy picture about the destruction of Pompeii. Stash had a part as Marius or Valerius or something—a rich wine merchant from Rome. He got five thousand dollars a

week, and he would be signed for three more pictures if
the producers liked him.

"It starts in a month?" Stash asked.

"Right," Nastar said. "But you leave for the coast
now. You got to work on your tan before they start to
shoot. I told them you had a nice tan. You know, you're
a Roman—you're wearing a white sheet all the time. Off
the shoulder. For the picture? A tan looks good."

"What am I going to live on for a month?" Stash
asked. "How am I going to get out there?"

"Listen," Nastar said. "You take my car, the one
you had in the country with Brenda. You drive it out
there. Then you sell it. Here." He gave Stash a piece of
paper with a name and an address written on it. "That's a
friend of mine in Los Angeles—from my country. He
sells cars out there. You take the car to him, he'll buy it,
he'll help you find a place to live cheap until the picture
starts."

"Why?" Stash asked, for the first time. For the last
time.

"Why what?" Nastar asked him.

"This guy. Why should he do all that?"

"Because I told him to," Nastar said. "I talked to
him."

"Well, look," Stash said. "I can't pay you for
the car."

"You pay me when they pay you," Nastar said.
"Five thousand bucks a week. A *week*, right? Hah. I guess
you can pay me."

Nastar finished his juice, set his glass down, and
looked at Stash across the table. "This is the big one for
you, Neville," he said. "You could hit. It doesn't happen
to everybody, you know. It is happening to you. But

you've got to stand up and say, okay, take me. You can do that, can't you?"

Stash and Nastar left the restaurant and walked together up Broadway. Stash was going to go, of course. There was no reason he shouldn't go any time, really—that day, the next.

"So," Nastar asked Stash, "what happened up in the country last month? What did you do?"

"Oh," Stash said. "Nothing. Nothing." He was thinking about all that was going to happen to him, and how soon. "We saw her sister's baby, you know, for his birthday?"

"Her sister's baby?" Nastar asked.

"Yeah," Stash said. "You know, with her husband and the rest."

"Oh, sure," Nastar said.

Two days later Stash had Nastar's car. He'd put all his things in the back and parked in front of the building where Brenda lived. Seven o'clock on a Sunday morning, and Stash and Brenda were down on the street beside the car. The sun was shining on the buildings and turning them the colors of oranges and lemons.

"I wanted to say, Stan," Brenda said, "I always thought you didn't have a good time up at home. I'm sorry if that's so. I didn't want to go alone, is all."

"Wait a minute," Stash said. "Sure, I did. Sure, I had a good time."

"Well, anyway," Brenda said. "I'm sorry if you didn't."

"Well," Stash said. "You know. I guess I'm a city guy."

"I guess so," Brenda said.

"Like you," Stash said. "You're a city guy, too, now."

"I don't think so," she said.

Stash found his way across the Hudson River and headed west. That early in the morning nobody was around.

"I had maybe seventy-five dollars, but I had that for gas, so I slept in the car and I ate—I don't know— potato chips.

"I left New York in early December," he said. "And I didn't really know how long it was going to take to drive to California. Nastar said seven or eight days. But out west it was winter already, and I was in this snowstorm that went on for three days. I got stuck in Cheyenne, Wyoming, in this snowstorm. We were all in this old hotel, me and all these totally crazy people who were traveling: cowboys and farmers and guys selling tractors. Worse than New York. Well, they heard I was going to be in a picture and needed a tan. How was I going to get a tan there in Wyoming in a blizzard? So they got these lights from the lobby, from the rooms, and I sat there in the bar with the lights on me and all these farmers and cowboys and guys buying drinks. I don't think it did any good."

Stash was silent. For the last time he turned in his seat on the parapet and looked off over the bay, to the distant lights of the town. "You know," he told us, "I think a lot about Nastar Radash. I paid him back when the picture started, for the car. And then pretty soon I got another agent because it didn't make sense for me to have a New York agent when I was going to be, you know, based in California. Nastar was connected out there, but not as well as Joel, the guy I got.

"But Nastar really was a wonderful, generous guy, I think. I look at what he did for me. Everything I needed, he knew about and he got. I didn't know what I ought to do, but he did. And now, you know, I owe him a lot, and I'm glad of it. I'm glad to owe him. I had a good life, I mean, I made some money, I had some fun, good friends. I traveled, I almost always had work, and I never had to work too hard. And totally because of Nastar Radash—one guy.

"And it was Brenda that got me and Nastar together, I don't forget," Stash said. He laughed. "Nastar was so cagey about her. Once years later I was in New York and I looked Nastar up like I always did when I was in town—but I was hardly ever in town.

"Anyway, I took Nastar to lunch at a good place, no juice bar. That place down in the basement. And we had a couple of drinks. I knew Brenda wasn't working for Nastar any more, so I asked him if he knew where she was, and he said he thought she'd gone back, you know, to Vermont."

"Did she?" my wife asked me then, interrupting Stash.

"No," I said.

"So then I asked Nastar," Stash said. "I said, you know—what was the story on you and her, anyway?"

"And Nastar said to me, what story? What do you mean?"

Mendez Vargas rose from his seat and, taking the hand of his young wife, drew her up from hers. "My friends," he said to us. "It is past midnight."

"Oh," Stash said. "I'm sorry. I'm a little drunk and totally boring. I apologize."

"Darling, no," said Antoinette Blakemore.

"Darling, yes," Stash said. "I know when I'm drunk, and I know when I'm boring. Anyway, I'm off to bed." He slid heavily down from the parapet. "My host, many thanks," Stash said to young Mendez Vargas.

"Señor Mowbray," said Mendez Vargas.

Stash left us, and Antoinette followed him. Shortly Mendez Vargas and his lady said goodnight. My wife and I remained on the terrace in the warm dark, but only for a few minutes. We too were sleepy.

"I'll never get used to it," my wife said. "You knew all those people, the ones from your town: the girl, and her sister, and her sister's husband. You knew all about them. You knew them all."

"Well," I said. "You have to understand: it's such a little place."

Copyedited by SOHO PRESS.

Design by Frank Lamacchia.

Production by H. Dean Ragland, Cobb/Dunlop
Publishers Services, Incorporated.

Set in Garamond by Kachina, Inc.

Printed by Maple Vail on acid free paper, and
manufactured with sewn bindings.